ALASTAR
WHERE DEATH AWAITS
Ron Trentham

Alastar Manor

Where Death Awaits

Copyright © 2024 by R Trentham

All rights reserved. No part of this book may be reproduced or used in any manner without written permission of the copyright owner except for the use of quotations in a book review.

First Edition, November 2024

This is a work of fiction. Names, characters, places, and incidents either are products of the author's imagination or are used fictitiously. Any resemblance to actual persons, living or dead, events, or locales is entirely coincidental.

Table of Contents

Chapter 1: Alastar Manor 1
Chapter 2: Renovations 4
Chapter 3: First Day 8
Chapter 4: First Night 13
Chapter 5: A Call for Help 18
Chapter 6: Old Friends, New Shadows 22
Chapter 7: Unspoken Tensions 26
Chapter 8: An Unexpected Guest 30
Chapter 9: Dreams Begin 35
Chapter 10: Into Town 40
Chapter 11: Trapped by the Storm 44
Chapter 12: Cody's Nightmare 48
Chapter 13: Voices Unseen 53
Chapter 14: Sarah 57
Chapter 15: Sam 61
Chapter 16: Alen 65
Chapter 17: A House That Watches 69
Chapter 18: House of Shadows 76
Chapter 19: Fractures 81
Chapter 20: All Hell Breaks Loose 86
Chapter 21: Splintered 91
Chapter 22: Shattered 96
Chapter 23: Shadows in the Past 101
Chapter 24: Alone 106
Chapter 25: The Wrong Sam 109
Chapter 26: Something New 113
Chapter 27: Cody's Fear 117
Chapter 28: Cody's Descent 123
Chapter 29: Helen Morrow 128
Chapter 30: A Way Out 133
Chapter 31: The House Closes In 138

Chapter 32: Unseen Shadows..143
Chapter 33: The Changing House...148
Chapter 34: The Return..152
Chapter 35: Sam and Thomas..154
Chapter 36: The Horrors Unveiled 158
Chapter 37: False Salvation 161
Chapter 38: Unraveling Fear...165
Chapter 39: Thomas Story 170
Chapter 40: The Wrong Hallway..174
Chapter 41: The Demon's Lair 178
Chapter 42: The Demon's Game..182
Chapter 43: Cody and Thomas 188
Chapter 44: The Curse of Alastar Manor..192
Chapter 45: A Silent Record...197
Chapter 46: The Attic..203
Chapter 47: Descent 210
Chapter 48: The Final Hour...215
Chapter 49: Epilogue: A New Beginning 224
Acknowledgement 228
Other Books by Ron Trentham...229

Chapter 1: Alastar Manor

The front door of Alastar Manor creaked open like it was alive and didn't want to let Danny in. It was like it was saying, "Who the hell are you and why are you bothering me?" The place had that damp, musty smell of a house that's been abandoned for a long, long time. Danny stepped inside, letting the door slam shut behind him, and it muffled the sound of the rain like it was trying to keep the outside world out.

"Jesus," he thought, wrinkling his nose, "it smells like a freakin' crypt in here."

The townies had warned him about the place being a wreck, and they weren't kidding. The floorboards whined under his boots, and there was a weird heaviness in the air that didn't just come from dust bunnies. Something felt off, like the house had been waiting for someone—but not him.

Danny was only there to check if it was worth fixing up. His boss had a thing for old, creepy houses and thought they could make a buck flipping them. But as Danny moved through the dark hallways, he couldn't shake the feeling that he wasn't the only one there.

"Okay," he murmured to himself, trying to sound braver than he felt, "just do your job. Check the foundation, make sure it's not going to collapse, and get out."

The flashlight barely cut through the darkness as he walked into what might have once been a dining room. The chandelier was crooked, and dust was piled on the table so thick it looked like it hadn't been touched in ages. As he moved across the floor, the dust clouds made him feel like he was disturbing something ancient.

And that's when he felt it—a cold chill that had nothing to do with the weather. It was like someone—or something—was watching him. His heart raced, and he swung the light around the room. Nothing.

"Come on, Danny," he whispered, trying to convince himself he wasn't losing it, "just a drafty old house."

But when he turned back, a door at the far end of the room had cracked open, just a sliver. "Hello?" he called out, his voice echoing in the vast emptiness. The silence was so thick it was almost a reply.

He approached the door, nudging it open with his foot. The light from his flashlight spilled into the hallway beyond, but there was nothing there—just more darkness. He laughed nervously. "You're just jumping at shadows, man."

As he turned to leave, the air around him grew colder, and the house groaned like it was alive. And then he heard it—a whisper. "Come closer..."

Danny spun around, his flashlight beam dancing across the room. "What the hell?"

The whisper grew louder, turning into a voice that seemed to come from nowhere. "Come closer..." "Who's there?" he yelled into the darkness, his heart racing.

Then, out of the corner of his eye, he saw it. A man, dressed like he'd just walked out of a '50s movie, standing in the shadows. Those eyes, though—sunken and empty, staring right at him.

"What do you want?" Danny managed to croak out.

The figure took a step closer, the sneer on its face growing more menacing. "Get out now!"

Danny's legs finally kicked into gear, and he sprinted back through the house, the creature's footsteps echoing behind him. The walls felt like they were closing in, and the floorboards seemed to trip him up. He stumbled into the front hall, the door seemingly miles away.

"Please, no," he whispered as he heard the creature's voice again, closer this time, "I'm going!"

FINALLY, THE DOOR SWUNG open, and he fell into the rain, gulping in the fresh, wet air.

He didn't stop running until he reached his truck. Looking back, the door to Alastar Manor was wide open, beckoning him to come back inside.

But Danny had had enough. He wasn't going back in there. Not tonight.

Robert Morrow stood there and watched as Danny ran out of the house, at least this night the house would not feed.

Chapter 2: Renovations

Alen pulled his truck up next to the realtor's car, gravel crunching under the tires as he parked. Alastar Manor sat in front of him, big and beat-up, looking even worse in person than it had in the photos. He knew it was rough, but that was the reason he was interested. The place was dirt cheap for its size, and he was sure he could fix it up and flip it for a nice profit.

He stepped out of the truck, zipping his jacket against the cold as he took in the house. The roof sagged, the windows were cracked, and the porch looked ready to collapse, but all Alen saw was potential. A mess, yeah, but one he could turn into something valuable.

The realtor, a woman in her thirties with that overly chipper saleswoman vibe, stepped out of her car at the same time, smiling as she walked over. "Alen! So glad you made it."

"Yeah," he said, nodding toward the house. "Wanted to see it up close. The pictures didn't exactly do it justice."

She laughed, a little too bright. "Right? Well, it's got potential, that's for sure. With a bit of work, this place could really shine."

"Yeah, I can see that," Alen said, glancing up at the cracked windows. "Just gotta tear half of it apart first."

The realtor smiled, trying to stay positive. "Come on, I'll show you around."

Alen followed her up the front steps, the wood creaking under his boots. The door groaned as she pushed it open, and a gust of stale air hit him in the face, thick with dust and that damp, musty smell old houses always seemed to have. He wrinkled his nose but stepped inside without hesitation.

"Smells like it's been sitting empty for years," he muttered, taking a look around the massive foyer.

"Yeah, it's been a while since anyone lived here," she said quickly. "But once it's aired out and cleaned up, it'll feel a lot better."

The foyer was huge, with high ceilings and a grand staircase that wound up to the second floor. Dust covered everything, and the floorboards creaked under their feet, but Alen could already see the potential. The house had good bones, even if it was falling apart.

"Place is big," Alen said, running a hand over the banister. "This staircase'll look great once it's refinished. Still solid."

The realtor smiled like she was relieved he wasn't immediately running for the door. "Exactly! That's the thing about these old houses, they're built to last. They just need a little TLC."

"Yeah," Alen muttered, stepping into the living room. "And a shitload of money."

The living room was in rough shape. The windows were fogged up with grime, and the wallpaper was peeling at the edges. Dust hung in the air, and a chandelier dangled crooked from the ceiling, missing half its crystals. Alen walked through the room, taking it all in. The place needed work, no doubt, but he wasn't scared off.

"This'll clean up nice," he said, knocking on one of the windows. "Gotta replace the glass, but the frames are still good. Open up this space, get some light in here, and it'll look ten times better."

The realtor nodded enthusiastically. "That's what I was thinking! Once the light comes through, this room will feel completely different."

Alen glanced at the old furniture still sitting around, covered in dust. "What's the deal with the furniture? They just leave all this behind?"

She shifted awkwardly. "Yeah, the last owners... well, they had some trouble keeping up with things. I guess they left in a bit of a hurry."

"Huh," Alen said, stepping past an old chair. "Well, I'll probably toss most of it. This room's got good bones, though. Could be a real showpiece once it's cleaned up."

They moved into the dining room next, where a long, dust-covered table sat in the middle of the room, surrounded by old chairs. The wallpaper was curling away from the walls, and water stains were spreading across the ceiling. It looked worse than it was, though, at least to Alen.

He ran a hand over the table, wiping away some of the dust. "This room's solid. Needs work, but the space is good. Fix the roof, get rid of the leaks, and it'll be fine."

The realtor nodded. "Yep, the house just needs someone who can see past the surface."

Alen gave her a quick grin. "That's why I'm here."

Next was the kitchen, and it was rough. Rusted appliances, stained countertops, and cabinets hanging on for dear life. The whole thing needed to be gutted, but Alen wasn't bothered by that. It was just part of the job.

"Yeah, I'll rip all this out," he said, shaking his head. "Start fresh. Once it's done, the kitchen'll add a ton of value."

"That's the plan," she said, smiling. "This space has so much potential once you update it."

They moved down a narrow hallway lined with old portraits. Alen didn't look too closely at the stiff, faded faces staring out from the walls, but something about the place felt colder as they went deeper into the house. The realtor opened the door to one of the bedrooms, showing off a dark, dusty room with heavy curtains drawn tight over the windows. The bedframe stood in the middle, empty, and the whole place looked like it had been abandoned in a hurry.

"Who the hell lived here last?" Alen muttered, rubbing the back of his neck. "Feels like they just took off and left everything behind."

The realtor gave a small, awkward laugh. "Yeah, they... had some issues. But it's nothing you can't handle, right?"

Alen nodded, glancing around the room. "Yeah, no problem. A little demo, some new finishes, and this place'll look brand new."

They headed back toward the staircase, and the realtor hesitated, flipping through her papers. "Oh, one more thing," she said, lowering her voice a little. "The last contractor we had here? He didn't stay long."

Alen raised an eyebrow. "What happened?"

She shrugged. "He, uh, said he kept hearing things. Seeing shadows. Thought the place was haunted."

Alen chuckled. "Haunted, huh? People really buy into that shit?"

The realtor smiled nervously. "Some people do, I guess. Old houses make noise, you know?"

"Yeah, I know," Alen said, glancing back up the stairs. "He probably just wasn't up for the job."

She looked relieved. "I'm glad you're not scared off."

Alen took one last look around, eyes lingering on the dark corners of the house. It was old, yeah, and a little creepy, but nothing he couldn't handle. He'd flipped worse.

"Nah," he said with a shrug. "I'm not worried. This place'll be great once it's done."

Chapter 3: First Day

Alen stood in the doorway of Alastar Manor, hands on his hips, staring at the shitshow in front of him. Sunlight cut through the dirty windows, casting pale streaks across the floor, but it didn't do much to soften the place. The smell of old wood, dust, and something... wet, maybe mold, clung to the air.

"Fuck," he muttered under his breath, pulling on his gloves. "Time to get started."

He wasn't here to admire the decay. He was here to clean this mess up, rip out the old, and make something new. The furniture was first. Had to be. It looked like it'd been sitting there for decades, probably hadn't seen a good dusting since before he was born. Alen grabbed a busted chair, fabric torn and sagging, and dragged it toward the door.

CREAK.

He froze. That didn't sound like just the floor. He glanced back over his shoulder. Nothing moved. The air was heavy, still.

"Old fuckin' house," he muttered, shaking it off. He knew better. Old houses made all kinds of noises. Wood warps, floors settle. That's all it was. He wasn't gonna let a creak freak him out.

He kicked open the front door, dragging the chair outside. The cold air hit him, clean and sharp, cutting through the thick mustiness that clung to the inside of the house. He tossed the chair onto the pile and wiped the sweat off his forehead with the back of his glove. His breath came out in quick bursts, clouding the air in front of him. Maybe he was working too fast, trying to get too much done too soon.

"Take it easy," he muttered to himself.

Back inside, the silence hit him harder. Too quiet. Not the peaceful kind of quiet, either. It was thick, pressing against his ears like he'd just walked into a cave. The kind of quiet that makes you feel like something's waiting to fill it.

"Just a house," he whispered, like saying it out loud would calm his nerves.

He grabbed the next piece of furniture, a beat-up coffee table, and started hauling it toward the door. The whole room felt like it was watching him, like the walls were closing in a little more with every step he took. His fingers tightened around the edges of the table as his heart started to beat a little faster.

Then he saw it. Out of the corner of his eye.

A shadow in the far corner of the room. Darker than it should've been. It was just... sitting there, like it didn't belong.

He stopped moving. The table hung heavy in his hands, but he barely noticed. He was staring, his breath catching in his throat.

"C'mon," he muttered, shaking his head, forcing himself to blink. "You're losing it, man."

The shadow didn't move, but something about it was wrong. Too dark. Too still. He felt a shiver crawl up his spine, a cold tickle that settled at the back of his neck. His hands felt clammy inside his gloves.

Get a grip, he told himself. *It's just the light messing with you.*

He hauled the table outside, dumped it on the pile, and leaned against the doorframe for a minute, rubbing the tension out of his neck. He hadn't even been here half a day, and the place was already getting under his skin.

"Don't be a pussy," he muttered. "It's a house. A run-down, piece-of-shit house."

But as soon as he stepped back inside, that feeling hit him again. The stillness. The quiet. He could feel his pulse in his ears, like the house was listening to it. He took a deep breath and grabbed the last chair, dragging it across the floor.

That's when he heard it.

Footsteps. Faint, soft, like someone walking upstairs. He froze, muscles tensing up, gripping the chair a little too tight. The footsteps weren't random. They had a rhythm to them. Someone walking.

Alen's mouth went dry. He listened, not moving a muscle. One footstep, then another. Slow. Deliberate.

He swallowed hard, his heart starting to pound in his chest. "Okay, okay," he whispered. "Old house. Just the house."

But the footsteps kept coming, each one heavier, like they were getting closer. Upstairs, then down the hall. Right above him.

He set the chair down, the sound too loud in the silence. His hands were shaking as he pulled off his gloves. "This is fuckin' stupid," he muttered. "No one's here. It's just the house settling."

But he wasn't so sure. His gut was twisted up, that instinctual feeling kicking in. He grabbed his flashlight and flicked it on, the beam cutting through the dim hallway as he headed toward the stairs.

Each step he took felt heavier, like the air was thicker the higher he went. His boots hit the wooden stairs with a dull thud, echoing louder than it should've. The cold hit him hard as he reached the second floor, sharp and biting.

"Jesus," he muttered, shining the light down the hall.

It looked longer than he remembered. The shadows stretched out like they were crawling into every corner. He took a slow breath, squaring his shoulders, and started walking. The footsteps had stopped now, but the silence was worse.

He reached the first door, the one with the heavy curtains and the old bedframe sitting in the middle of the room. The flashlight beam swept across the empty space, cutting through the dark, but nothing moved.

"Just your fuckin' imagination," he muttered, lowering the light.

He turned to leave, but before he could take a step, something thudded behind him. Alen spun around, heart racing. The beam of the flashlight flickered across the bedframe.

It had moved.

"Fuck," he whispered, staring at the bed. "That wasn't like that."

He took a step back, then another. His palms were slick with sweat inside his gloves, his breath coming faster now. The bed didn't move again, but the air in the room felt different. Thicker. Like it was pressing in on him.

Alen backed up into the hall, keeping his eyes on the doorway. He wasn't sure what the hell had just happened, but he didn't like it. His gut was tight, his skin buzzing with that instinctive *get the hell out* feeling.

But he couldn't leave. This was his place now. He had work to do.

"Old house," he muttered. "That's all it is. Old fuckin' house."

He headed back downstairs, moving quicker than he wanted to admit, but his pulse was still thudding in his ears. The second his boots hit the first floor, he exhaled, finally letting his shoulders relax a little. But he didn't feel right. Not anymore.

He stood there, catching his breath, staring up at the stairs. The shadows seemed thicker now. Darker. He didn't want to go back up there. Not yet.

Grabbing his gloves, Alen headed outside, tossing the last chair onto the pile. The cold air stung his face, but it felt better out here. Cleaner. Like he could breathe again.

He glanced back at the house, squinting at the windows. The shadows inside seemed to move, shift, but maybe that was just his eyes messing with him.

"Place is fucking with me," he muttered. "But I'm not goin' anywhere."

He wasn't about to let a few creaks and a bed frame scare him off. He had money sunk into this place, and he wasn't about to run at the first weird thing he saw.

Grabbing his tools, Alen headed back inside. He'd figure it out. One way or another.

Chapter 4: First Night

Alen dumped the last busted chair onto the pile, rubbing the back of his neck as he looked out at the night. The sky had turned that deep purple, the cold biting harder now. He stretched his arms, cracking his knuckles, feeling the dull ache in his muscles. It had been a long day. Good work, but his body was already complaining.

"Yeah, that'll do," he muttered, rolling his shoulders as he headed back inside. The door gave a heavy thud when he shut it behind him, the sound echoing through the empty rooms.

The cold followed him in, settling in the air like a heavy blanket. The place was quiet. Too damn quiet. No hum of traffic, no people, just this thick silence that pressed in on him. It felt unnatural. He rubbed his hands together, trying to shake off the chill that had already wormed its way under his skin.

He kicked off his boots and padded barefoot across the wood floor, his steps echoing as he made his way to the small room he'd picked to crash in. A sleeping bag, his jacket for a pillow, and a weak little lamp he'd set up in the corner. Not much, but better than freezing his ass off in some overpriced motel.

Alen stretched out on the sleeping bag, pulling it tight up to his chest. The cold air hit his face, sharp, and the shadows in the corners of the room seemed to shift, heavy and thick. He exhaled, long and slow, staring up at the ceiling.

"You're fine," he muttered, almost like he was trying to convince himself. "It's just a house."

He closed his eyes, letting the exhaustion settle into his bones. His breathing slowed, the day's work catching up with him. His body was dead tired, his head starting to drift off, but just as he was about to slip under, something cracked.

Snap.

Alen's eyes shot open. That wasn't the usual groan of an old house. That was sharper, like something had snapped under pressure. He froze, his heart kicking up a notch as he listened.

Another sound. This time a soft creak, like a footstep, slow and deliberate.

"What the hell..." he whispered.

He sat up, grabbing his flashlight, flicking it on. The weak beam of light cut through the dim room, landing on the door to the hallway. Nothing. He stayed still, listening, but the house had gone silent again.

Then, just outside the door, the floor groaned under a heavy weight. One step, then another, slow as hell, like someone dragging their feet.

His mouth went dry. He kept the flashlight steady, aimed at the door. His pulse was thumping so loud he swore whoever—or whatever—was out there could hear it.

Alen forced himself to stand, feet cold against the floor as he moved toward the door. His gut twisted, but he wasn't about to let some noises freak him out. It was just the house. Old wood and empty rooms made noise, that's all. That had to be it.

He stepped into the hallway, his bare feet silent on the wood. The air out here was colder, sharp enough to sting his skin. It smelled stale, like old wood, but there was something else. Something off, like dampness, or maybe mold.

"Okay..." he muttered, shining the light toward the stairs.

The stairs groaned softly, like they'd been disturbed. He stood there, heart racing, staring at the dark outline of the staircase. The light barely touched it, just enough to show that nothing was there. But the silence felt... heavy, like the house was holding its breath.

"You're hearing shit," he told himself, but the knot in his stomach told a different story.

He stood there for a minute longer, his flashlight shaking in his hand. Then, slowly, he took a step toward the stairs. The wood under his feet creaked, loud in the quiet. He stopped, waiting, but there was nothing. No more steps. No more sounds.

"Fuckin' floors," he muttered, trying to shake off the unease crawling up his spine.

Alen took another step, then another, each one slow, deliberate. The stairs groaned under his weight, but the sound was different this time. Lower, like something was bending under the pressure, like the house was adjusting to him.

He stopped at the base of the staircase, shining the light up into the blackness above. The air was thick, cold, and for a second, he swore the shadows moved. Just a flicker, a shift, like something pulled back out of sight.

He swallowed hard. His throat was dry as hell, and his skin felt prickly, like static was creeping up his arms. Every part of him was telling him to turn around, go back to the sleeping bag, and write this off as a bad dream.

But he couldn't. He'd spent too much time here already, invested too much. He wasn't about to let a few bumps in the night chase him out.

"Get a grip," he muttered, taking the first step.

The wood groaned, a long, drawn-out sound, like it was complaining about the weight. Alen winced, pausing, then kept going. Each step felt heavier, the cold biting deeper as he climbed. When he reached the top, the air hit him hard, sharp and stale. He swept the flashlight down the hallway, the light barely pushing through the thick shadows clinging to the walls.

Everything looked normal, but that gut feeling? It was telling him something wasn't right. His heartbeat pounded in his ears, his breathing shallow as he moved toward the first door on the left—the one with the heavy curtains. The bedframe was in there.

He reached the door, stopping just outside, listening. His fingers tightened around the flashlight, his pulse a drumbeat in his head. He nudged the door open with his elbow, the hinges creaking loud in the silence.

The room was cold as hell, colder than before, the air thick and still. His flashlight swept across the floor, the walls, and finally, the bed.

He froze.

The bedframe had shifted.

Just an inch or two, but enough that it wasn't where it had been before. His breath caught in his throat, his skin crawling. He stood there, staring, heart pounding in his chest.

"No fuckin' way," he whispered, backing up a step. "I didn't touch that."

The room didn't move. The bed didn't shift again. But something in the air had changed, something he couldn't put his finger on.

Alen took another step back, then another, until he was back in the hallway. His hands were slick with sweat, the flashlight trembling in his grip. He couldn't explain what he'd just seen, and that bothered him more than anything. This wasn't how things were supposed to go.

He swallowed hard, his breath shaky as he turned toward the stairs. Each step creaked under his weight as he hurried back down, not bothering to be quiet anymore. When he reached the bottom, he stopped, leaned against the wall, and tried to catch his breath.

The house had gone quiet again. But it wasn't the peaceful kind of quiet. It was the kind that crawled under your skin, made you feel like you weren't alone.

He wiped his forehead, slick with sweat despite the cold. His hands shook as he rubbed them together, trying to get some warmth back, but it wasn't working.

"What the hell's goin' on here?" he muttered, pacing the room.

He glanced back up at the stairs, his chest tight, but there was no way he was going back up there. Not tonight. Not after what he'd seen.

Alen grabbed his sleeping bag and dragged it into the living room, closer to the door. He wasn't running, but he sure as hell wasn't spending the night upstairs either.

As he settled down, the shadows in the corners seemed darker, deeper. But he wasn't ready to admit that the house was getting to him. Not yet.

Chapter 5: A Call for Help

Alen sat on the edge of his sleeping bag, phone in hand, staring at the dark corners of the room. His breath puffed out in short clouds, hanging in the freezing air, but it wasn't just the cold that had him on edge. The house felt... wrong. He hadn't slept worth a damn in days. Every time he closed his eyes, it was like the house was waiting to fuck with him—those creaks, those goddamn footsteps. The bed. He still couldn't get over how that thing had just *moved*.

He wiped a hand over his face, tired and frustrated. His thumb hovered over Sam's number on the screen. He hated feeling like he was losing it, but fuck, he needed someone here. He needed *Sam* here.

"Shit," he muttered and tapped the call button.

The phone rang a few times, and Alen found himself pacing the cold floor as he waited. Sam picked up after a few rings, voice thick with sleep.

"Alen? Dude, it's not even seven. What the hell's up?"

Alen rubbed the back of his neck, already feeling stupid for calling. "Yeah, I know, man, sorry. Look, you busy this week?"

There was a pause. He could hear Sam moving around, probably trying to wake himself up. "No, not really. Why?"

Alen took a breath, feeling that weird tension knot up in his stomach again. "I could use some help out here. You know, with the house. Thought maybe you could come stay for a bit. Free food, free beer, place to crash..."

Sam chuckled, though it was clear he still wasn't fully awake. "You need *help*? Didn't think you'd ever admit that. What's going on? You sound off."

"I'm just tired," Alen said, rubbing his temples. "This place is kicking my ass. It's bigger than I thought, and... I dunno, I'm sick of being out here alone. You know?"

Another pause. Alen could hear the faint sound of Sam moving again, probably getting out of bed. "Yeah, I hear you. Free food and beer, huh? That's all I get?"

Alen forced a laugh. "C'mon, man. I'll owe you one, big time. Just need some company out here."

Sam sighed, and Alen could almost picture him rubbing his face, that familiar smirk probably starting to form. "Alright, fine. I'll pack up and head over later today. But you definitely owe me for this."

Alen smiled, feeling a small weight lift off his chest. "Yeah, I know. Thanks, man."

Sam pulled up to the house that afternoon, the rumble of his old truck breaking the silence that had settled over the place. Alen was already standing on the porch, hands shoved into his jacket pockets, watching as Sam climbed out of the driver's seat.

"Damn, this place looks even shittier in person," Sam called out, slamming the truck door shut. He stretched his arms over his head, showing off his broad shoulders, his muscles flexing under his shirt. Sam had always been a good-looking bastard—handsome in that rugged way, with dark stubble that he never bothered to shave clean and a jawline that women went nuts over. His arms looked like they were built from years of actual labor, not just gym work. A guy who could charm people without even trying.

Alen shook his head, trying to keep the mood light. "Yeah, well, it's my shithole now. Welcome to Alastar Manor."

Sam grabbed his duffel bag from the truck bed and slung it over his shoulder, walking up the steps to meet Alen. He gave the house a once-over, his eyebrows raised. "You weren't kidding. This place is straight-up creepy as hell. You sure you don't have, like, a family of ghosts waiting to greet me at the door?"

Alen forced a grin. "If they are, they've been quiet... so far."

Sam rolled his eyes. "Well, if they start throwing shit around, I'm outta here. I didn't sign up for *that*."

Inside, the air hit Sam hard. "Jesus, it's freezing in here, man. You trying to turn this place into a meat locker or what?"

"Yeah, I know," Alen muttered, rubbing his hands together as they walked down the hallway. "Drafts, I guess. Old house problems."

Sam set his bag down near the kitchen, glancing around at the cracked walls and worn floorboards. "You really are in over your head with this one, huh?"

Alen leaned against the counter, feeling a tightness in his chest that had nothing to do with the cold. "Yeah, you could say that."

Sam cracked open a beer from the fridge, leaning against the counter. "So, what's really going on? You didn't call me just 'cause you need help with renovations. You've been doing this shit for years on your own. Something else is up."

Alen hesitated, glancing at the shadows in the corner of the room. He rubbed his hands together, trying to warm them, but it wasn't just the cold bothering him. "I... I don't know, man. I've just been hearing shit. Seeing things. It's... weird."

Sam raised an eyebrow, taking a sip of his beer. "Weird how?"

Alen swallowed, running a hand through his hair. "Footsteps. Late at night. Doors that won't stay closed. Cold spots that follow me around, and I swear to you, the fucking bed upstairs moved on its own. I'm not making this up."

Sam stared at him for a beat, beer halfway to his mouth. "You serious?"

Alen nodded, feeling that tightness in his chest again. "I wouldn't drag you out here if I wasn't."

For a moment, Sam didn't say anything. He set his beer down, leaning forward. "So you think the place is haunted?"

Alen laughed, but it was hollow. "I don't *know*. Maybe? All I know is, it's fucked up, and it's getting worse."

Sam looked him over, eyes narrowing slightly. "Alright, well, lucky for you, I'm here now. If this ghost of yours shows up, we'll kick his ass together."

Alen snorted. "Yeah, sure. You can take first watch, then."

That night, after a couple beers and a lazy dinner of whatever was left in Alen's fridge, the two of them settled into the living room. Sam was sprawled out on the couch, scrolling through his phone, while Alen sat by the window, staring out at the pitch-black yard. The cold had only gotten worse as the night went on, settling into his bones like ice.

"You alright over there?" Sam asked, glancing up from his phone. "You've been staring out that window for, like, twenty minutes. You waiting for something to jump outta the bushes?"

Alen blinked, shaking himself out of his trance. "No, just... thinking."

"About what? The ghosts?"

Alen sighed, sitting back down next to Sam. "You'll see. This place... it gets under your skin."

Sam chuckled, but there was a hint of unease creeping into his voice. "Well, if it does, I'll punch it right back. Ain't scared of some creepy-ass house."

Alen wanted to laugh, wanted to feel the way Sam made things seem so easy. But that tight feeling in his chest wasn't going away. The house was watching them. He knew it. The shadows in the corners of the room seemed to pulse, like they were waiting for something, and Alen had a feeling that whatever was in this house was just getting started.

Chapter 6: Old Friends, New Shadows

Alen stood on the porch, arms crossed, watching the dust kick up as the SUV finally rolled down the driveway. It had taken long enough. The quiet had been eating at him all morning, the house too still for his liking. With Sam by his side, they'd barely scratched the surface of the work, and he needed the others now more than ever.

"Finally," Alen muttered, rubbing his hands together.

Sam glanced up from his phone, smirking. "Cody probably made them stop for coffee or something. Dude's gotta have his fix."

The SUV came to a stop next to Sam's truck, and the doors swung open. First out was Cody, of course—always first, always with that big grin plastered across his face like he was stepping into some grand adventure. He was lean, sharp, and a natural at making everything look easy, from his messy-but-somehow-stylish hair to his confident swagger.

"Holy shit, Alen," Cody said, pulling off his sunglasses and taking in the house. "You weren't kidding. This place looks like it's straight outta a horror movie. Where's the creepy old caretaker?"

Alen gave him a sarcastic grin. "You're looking at him."

Cody laughed, but there was genuine excitement in his eyes. "Man, I love it. You know I'm into this old house shit. Let's get inside before I start redesigning the whole front yard."

Cody was the kind of guy who had a knack for making things look good. In college, he'd been the one to lead all their DIY projects—whether it was turning their crappy student apartment into something halfway livable or convincing everyone to help paint his aunt's old cabin during spring break. He could turn something broken into something decent, and he loved every second of it.

Sam leaned against the porch railing, throwing Cody a nod. "Just don't get too comfortable. I'm not painting anything unless I'm drunk first."

Cody flashed a grin and gave Sam a playful nudge as he passed. "Drunk painting sounds like a plan, buddy."

Before they could get too far into their usual banter, Sarah climbed out of the driver's seat, already looking annoyed. She brushed her dark hair back into a tighter ponytail, scanning the house like she was already mentally measuring everything that needed fixing. Sarah had always been the practical one in the group, the one who could handle a sledgehammer just as well as a spreadsheet. She worked for a big architecture firm now, but before that, she'd spent summers with her dad flipping houses, learning how to lay tile, knock down walls, and—her least favorite—rewire electrical systems.

"Damn, Alen," Sarah said, walking up to the porch with a shake of her head. "You sure this place is even standing? I've seen buildings on the verge of collapse that look better than this."

"It's standing," Alen replied, grinning. "Barely, but it's standing."

Sarah sighed, hands on her hips, but Alen could see the spark in her eyes. He knew her well enough to tell she wasn't just here to help—she was already mentally planning the renovation. She was into it, whether she'd admit it or not.

"Well, it's got potential," she said, her voice softening just a bit. "We can make this place look decent again if we don't fall through the floor first."

Cody snorted. "I'm more worried about the roof caving in, honestly."

The banter felt easy, the tension of the house's looming presence pushed to the background for a moment. Having them here made it better. At least for now.

Inside, the house felt colder, but none of them seemed to notice. They all fell right into their roles, just like old times. Cody was already wandering through the foyer, running his hands along the banister. "Man, this place is gonna be killer once we fix it up. Can't wait to get started."

Alen followed him into the living room, where Sam had set up camp. The dust was thick, but the room had started to take shape. The old fireplace still looked like something out of a haunted Victorian novel, but it had character. The kind Cody would love to restore.

"I'm thinking we rip up the carpet, refinish the floors, and repaint the walls a deep blue. Make it moody but not too dark, you know?" Cody said, already in design mode.

Sarah rolled her eyes as she tossed her jacket over a dusty chair. "Easy there, Chip Gaines. We've got bigger problems than paint colors. Like, the wiring's probably older than all of us combined."

"And there's probably asbestos lurking somewhere," Cody added, dropping onto the couch with a grin. "If we don't get haunted, we'll get cancer."

Sarah glared at him. "Not helping, Cody."

Cody just shrugged. "What? I'm just saying."

Alen chuckled, watching them settle in. It was strange how much better it felt to have everyone here, even with the cold gnawing at the back of his neck. They made the place feel alive again. Less... suffocating.

"I'll take the wiring," Sarah said, already pulling a notebook from her bag. "We'll need to get in the walls at some point, but I'll check the main lines first."

"Yeah, and I'll figure out what to do with the upstairs bedrooms," Cody added. "They're big, but man, that furniture up there is ugly. It's like someone tried to mix Victorian and 70s. We gotta toss it."

Alen swallowed hard, remembering the way that bed had shifted the other night. "We'll deal with that later. For now, let's focus on the first floor."

Sam raised an eyebrow but said nothing. Alen hadn't mentioned the moving furniture to anyone yet. Not Cody. Not Sarah. Maybe he was just imagining it. Maybe.

As they got to work, the atmosphere inside the house started to shift. The excitement they'd brought with them dulled the edges of the creeping dread that had settled into Alen's bones since the first night. Cody and Sam started clearing out the front hallway, laughing as they tossed old furniture out onto the porch. Sarah disappeared into the kitchen, muttering about wiring, and Sam was trying to figure out the plumbing situation.

For a while, it felt... normal. Like they were just fixing up another old house, like they'd done a million times before.

But every now and then, Alen caught himself pausing, staring at the shadowed corners of the room. The air was thick, colder than it should've been, and every once in a while, he'd swear he heard something moving upstairs. Just a creak. Just the wind. But it didn't feel right.

"Yo, Alen!" Cody called from the front room, snapping him out of his thoughts. "You ordering that pizza or what? We didn't come out here to starve, man!"

Alen forced a grin. "Yeah, yeah. I'm on it."

He pulled out his phone and started dialing, but the draft that blew through the room was colder than before. The windows rattled in their frames, and for a split second, the room felt... wrong. Heavy.

He glanced up the stairs, and the hair on the back of his neck stood on end. Something about the way the shadows shifted up there made his stomach twist.

He shook it off and punched in the number for pizza. Nothing was wrong. It was just the house settling. That's all.

Chapter 7: Unspoken Tensions

Three days had passed, and things were starting to fall into place faster than expected. The house, despite looking like it had been abandoned for decades, had turned out to be in surprisingly good shape. The wiring was newer than it should've been, the walls were solid, and even the plumbing, though loud, didn't give them the headaches they were bracing for.

"Whoever lived here before us did most of the work for you," Sarah said, tossing an old, cracked plate into the trash as she wiped her hands. "Not that I'm complaining. I was ready for a shitshow, but this is kinda nice."

Alen glanced up from where he was working on the baseboards. "I'm not gonna argue with that. Still feels weird, though. Place looks ancient, but the guts are in good shape."

"Yeah, well, better weird than falling apart," Sarah said, checking her notes.

They'd all been on edge, but there was a sense of relief in knowing the house wasn't as broken as they'd first thought. But that relief didn't stop the chill that always seemed to settle into the walls, or the feeling that something was watching them when no one was looking.

Later that afternoon, Cody and Sarah were left alone in the kitchen, cleaning up the last bits of old junk from the cabinets and countertops. The sun was starting to dip, casting the room in a soft golden light, but the air was still too cold for the time of year. Cody wiped down the counter with a rag, sleeves rolled up to his elbows, but he was quieter than usual. His usual playful energy was muted, like something was bothering him.

Sarah paused, tossing another cracked cup into the trash. "Alright, out with it."

Cody blinked, glancing up. "Huh?"

"You've been weird all day. What's going on?" Sarah leaned against the counter, giving him a knowing look. "Is it about Sam?"

Cody hesitated, shrugging. "Yeah. Sorta."

"Sorta?" Sarah smirked, crossing her arms. "Come on, you're not fooling me. You've had a thing for him for, what, like forever?"

Cody let out a sigh, running a hand through his hair. "Yeah, I know. It's dumb. He's straight, though, so what's the point?"

Sarah raised an eyebrow. "You *sure* he's straight? People can surprise you."

Cody snorted. "Trust me. He's straight. Doesn't mean I don't wish he wasn't, but... it's just one of those things, you know? I've known for years, but I'm not gonna mess up our friendship by making shit weird."

Sarah's face softened, her teasing replaced by something more serious. "I get it. You've got history. But bottling that up forever doesn't sound fun either."

"Yeah, well," Cody said, wiping his hands on his jeans, "better to keep it buried than to deal with the fallout. I'd rather be his friend than risk screwing it all up."

Sarah nodded, leaning back against the counter. "I mean, you know him best. But still, you've been carrying that weight around for a long time. That's gotta suck."

Cody laughed, but it didn't reach his eyes. "It does. Especially being around him so much these last few days. Just seeing him doing his thing, being all... Sam. I dunno. It's harder than I thought it'd be."

Sarah gave him a sympathetic smile. "I feel for you, man. But you're strong. You'll figure it out."

Cody nodded, but the weight of it all still hung over him. It wasn't like he could flip a switch and stop feeling what he felt. Every time Sam made him laugh, or every time they worked together on something, it just deepened that part of him that wanted more. And that was the hardest part—*wanting more* when he knew it wasn't in the cards.

The conversation died down, and they worked in silence for a while, the sound of clattering dishes and the creak of old cabinet doors filling the room. Cody kept wiping down the counters, but his mind was on Sam, on the way he'd flash that grin when they worked together, or how easy it was for him to make everyone feel comfortable. Cody hated how much he noticed those little things.

"Anyway," Cody said, breaking the silence, "thanks for listening. I know it's dumb."

"It's not dumb," Sarah said, tossing another cracked plate into the trash. "It's life. But you're gonna be fine."

Cody gave her a small, grateful smile. "Yeah. I will."

Later, as the sun dipped below the horizon, the kitchen felt colder. The chill in the air was starting to creep back in, making the room feel more closed in than it had before. Cody rubbed his arms, frowning.

"Is it just me, or is it freezing in here?" he asked, glancing around.

Sarah looked up from what she was doing and nodded. "Yeah, it's been on and off since we got here. Something's not right with this place."

"You're telling me," Cody muttered, looking out the window. The shadows outside were long now, stretching across the yard like dark fingers. The house was still solid, but something about it felt *off*, like it was holding something back.

Alen and Sam came into the kitchen a few minutes later, beers in hand. Alen cracked open his bottle, handing one to Sam as they leaned against the counter.

"We've made a hell of a dent," Alen said, clinking his bottle against Sam's. "I wasn't expecting this much progress this fast."

"Yeah," Sam agreed, taking a swig of his beer. "This place isn't as bad as it looks. Almost feels like someone did half the work for us."

Cody couldn't help but smile at Sam, but it didn't quite reach his eyes. "Yeah, maybe. Or maybe the house is saving the worst for last."

Sam raised an eyebrow, grinning. "You expecting a horror show?"

Cody shrugged, rubbing the back of his neck. "Just feels like this place has got secrets it's not sharing yet."

Sarah rolled her eyes. "Cody's ghost radar is back on, folks."

Cody chuckled, but the unease in his stomach wasn't going away. "Yeah, well, when the house finally shows its cards, don't say I didn't warn you."

Alen laughed, but as the cold air thickened in the room, he couldn't help but feel like Cody might be right.

Chapter 8: An Unexpected Guest

Late afternoon sunlight stretched long across the front yard of Alastar Manor, casting everything in a dull, fading glow. The day felt like it was winding down, but the air inside the house was heavy and cold. No one mentioned it, but everyone felt it.

Cody tossed another cracked vase into the junk pile by the door. "Where the hell's everyone? Seems like folks are taking forever to get back."

Sarah, who was elbow-deep in a box of old books, smirked. "They're probably hiding somewhere. You know how it goes—people vanish the moment the heavy lifting starts."

Cody shook his head, wiping the dust off his hands. "We should find 'em, drag their asses back here."

"Or," Sarah added, "we lock them in the attic and let them deal with the creepy stuff up there."

Before anyone could continue the banter, a low voice cut through the stillness.

"Hello? Anybody here?"

Cody turned toward the gate, squinting into the sunlight. An old man stood near the entrance, his weathered skin pulled tight over his bones, a faded ball cap hiding his eyes. He looked like someone who'd spent more time outdoors than inside, his clothes worn but not dirty, like he didn't care much about how they looked.

Alen came around the side of the house, wiping his hands on his jeans. "Hey, uh, can I help you?"

The man didn't answer right away. He just stared up at the house like it had some kind of hold on him. After a long pause, he finally spoke, his voice rough and low. "Didn't think anyone'd bother with this place."

Alen nodded, trying to shake off the unease creeping up his spine. "Yeah, well, figured it was worth a shot. You from around here?"

The man nodded, still staring at the house. "Been around long enough. Seen this place go through plenty of owners. None of 'em stayed long, though."

Cody shot a glance at Sarah, but she just kept working, not buying into whatever creepy story was coming next.

"Why's that?" Alen asked, feeling the cold knot of unease tightening in his stomach.

The man finally looked at Alen, his eyes sharp beneath the brim of his cap. "Bad things happen in houses like this. You'll see."

The way he said it hit hard, sinking deeper than it should've. Alen's breath hitched, and before he could think of what to say next, the man tipped his cap and turned, walking slowly back down the driveway like he had nowhere else to be.

Cody let out a low breath, running a hand through his hair. "Okay, what the hell was that?"

"Just some local trying to freak us out," Sarah said, shaking her head. "Every small town's got their own version of that guy."

Alen didn't respond. He kept staring at the driveway, the man's words echoing in his head. *You'll see.* It felt like a promise, not just some old man's weird warning. Something about it wouldn't let go.

That night, Alen couldn't sleep. The room felt colder than usual, the kind of cold that sinks into your bones and won't let go. He tossed and turned, pulling the blankets tighter around him, but it wasn't just the cold keeping him awake.

Eventually, exhaustion pulled him under.

The dream came slowly, like stepping into a memory that wasn't his. He was walking through Alastar Manor, but it wasn't the broken, decaying version they were trying to fix up. This place was untouched, like it had been frozen in time—polished wood floors, fresh wallpaper, the kind of perfect detail that felt too pristine, too clean.

But the air was heavy. Thick. He could hear voices now. Not whispers—louder. Clearer.

Two men. Arguing.

Alen couldn't make out the words, but the feeling was there. Tension hung in the air like a storm about to break, thick and electric. His feet felt like they were sinking into the floor with every step, but he kept moving, even though he didn't want to.

The voices pulled him forward, deeper into the house.

He turned a corner and found himself in a bedroom he didn't recognize—everything perfectly in place, too perfect. On the edge of the bed, one man sat hunched over, head in his hands. His shoulders were shaking. There was something broken in the way he sat, like he was carrying the weight of the world and it was too much.

The other man stood near the window, staring out, fists clenched at his sides. Alen couldn't see his face—both of them were turned away from him—but he could feel the anger radiating off the one by the window. It filled the room, making the air feel too thick, too hard to breathe.

"Why did you tell him?" The voice was sharp, strained. The kind of anger that was holding back something darker. The man by the window didn't turn, but his words were cold, cutting. "You know what happens if they find out."

The man on the bed didn't answer right away. He just shook his head, hands gripping his hair. "I didn't mean to—"

"You didn't mean to?" The man by the window snapped, spinning around, his face twisted in anger. But when Alen tried to see him, his features blurred, like the dream wouldn't let him get too close. "You've ruined us."

The room seemed to close in around them, the walls pushing tighter. Alen's heart pounded in his chest, but his feet wouldn't move. He felt stuck there, like he was trapped in this moment with them.

"I didn't mean to tell," the man on the bed said, his voice breaking. "I just... I loved you. I thought..."

"Thought what?" The man by the window spat, stepping forward. His body was tense, hands balled into fists, shaking with barely contained rage. "You ruined everything."

The man on the bed finally looked up, but his face—Alen couldn't see it clearly. It was smudged, like a photo that had been dragged through water, blurring all the details. But Alen could feel his pain. It was in every inch of the room, suffocating.

"I loved you," the man whispered, his voice shattered and full of regret.

The room felt like it was caving in, the air too thick to breathe, the tension so sharp it felt like it was choking him. Alen wanted to move, wanted to scream, but his body wouldn't listen.

The man by the window stepped closer, his voice dropping to a dangerous whisper. "You shouldn't be here."

Alen's chest tightened. His throat felt like it was closing up, the words echoing in his head.

"You shouldn't be here."

Alen shot up in bed, gasping, his body drenched in sweat. His heart hammered in his chest, the cold air of the room biting at his skin. He looked around, his eyes darting to the shadows in the corners, half-expecting to see the two men still standing there, their anger still hanging in the air.

But the room was empty.

His breath came in shaky bursts, his pulse still pounding in his ears. He ran a hand over his face, trying to shake off the weight of the dream, but it clung to him, thick and sticky, like it didn't want to let go.

The clock on the nightstand glowed faintly—just past 3 a.m. Too late to fall back asleep, too early to be awake.

He sat there, staring at the shadows, the cold from the dream still settled deep in his bones.

And that whisper, still lingering in his mind.

You shouldn't be here.

Chapter 9: Dreams Begin

Alen hadn't told anyone about the dreams. He wasn't ready to deal with their looks—Cody's raised eyebrows, Sarah's sarcasm, Sam's laid-back "You're just overthinking it, man" attitude. The dreams weren't something he could brush off, though. They stuck to him like sweat, creeping into his mind even when he was awake. The worst part? They weren't just dreams anymore. Every time he closed his eyes, it felt like the house was *there*, pushing into his head, filling his sleep with cold, thick air, like it was suffocating him.

"Hey!" Cody's voice snapped him back to reality. Alen blinked, realizing he'd been staring at the same fucking spot on the wall for who knows how long. Cody stood there, arms crossed, frowning. "Dude, you alright? You've been zoning out all day."

"Yeah, yeah. I'm fine." Alen rubbed his eyes, trying to shake off the fog that had settled over him.

"Doesn't look like it." Cody grabbed a dusty old chair from the corner and gave it a half-hearted shove. "You've been acting weird, man. You look like you've seen some shit."

Alen tried to force a smile, but it felt tight. "Just tired. Haven't slept much."

"Tell me about it," Cody muttered, kicking the chair toward the junk pile. "This house is doing a real number on us. You'd better start getting some shut-eye before you go full Jack Nicholson on us."

Alen laughed, but it came out hollow. The truth was, he didn't want to sleep. Not when the house was in his dreams, too.

A couple of days went by in a blur. The cold had settled into the house, creeping into every room like it belonged there. Alen could feel it, deep in his bones, but he didn't say anything. What could he say? *Hey guys, the house is fucking with me*? They'd think he was losing it.

One night, they were all sitting in the living room, beers in hand, staring into the fire that was doing jack shit to warm the place up. The conversation was light, but it didn't feel real. They were all distracted, their words trailing off into the crackle of the flames.

"I don't like this place," Sarah said out of nowhere, her voice sharp. She looked around the room like she was searching for something. "I mean, it's in better shape than I expected, but... I don't know. There's something *wrong* here."

Cody raised an eyebrow, glancing between her and Alen. "Come on, it's just an old house. I mean, yeah, it's creepy as hell, but nothing we can't handle, right?"

"It's not that," Sarah said, shaking her head. "It feels like... like it's *watching* us. Like it's waiting for something."

Alen's chest tightened. He hadn't said anything about the dreams, about the way the house was starting to get under his skin, but Sarah's words hit way too close to home. He cleared his throat. "Yeah. I've been feeling that, too. Like it's not just us in here."

They all fell silent, the room growing heavier. Even the fire seemed quieter, like it was listening, too.

Alen didn't even bother trying to sleep that night. He lay in bed, staring at the ceiling, knowing what was waiting for him if he closed his eyes. The house had become a living thing, its presence pushing into his head, suffocating him. He could feel the cold air crawling under his skin, like fingers digging into his bones. The silence was thick, pressing against his chest.

And when he finally drifted off, the dream swallowed him whole.

He was back in the hallway. The air was so cold it burned, like ice in his lungs. The walls stretched out in front of him, too long, too narrow, like the house was trying to trap him. He could hear the voices again—low, muffled, angry—but this time, they were more than just noise. He could feel the hatred in the air, thick and suffocating, like it was pressing down on him.

His legs felt heavy, like he was wading through water, but he kept moving, pulled forward by something he didn't want to see. The door loomed ahead, taller and darker than it should've been. He didn't want to go in, but his feet wouldn't stop. They were dragging him, step by painful step, closer to that room.

He pushed the door open, and the cold hit him like a punch in the gut. The room was wrong. The bed was made, the curtains still swayed, but the air was filled with something else—something dark, *alive*. It crawled over his skin, making his heart pound in his chest.

He saw them then—two men. One was standing by the window, his back tense, his fists clenched. The other sat on the bed, head in his hands, his shoulders shaking like he was about to fall apart. They didn't look at Alen. It was like he wasn't even there. But the tension between them was real. It was choking the air.

"You told him." The man by the window spoke first, his voice like ice. He didn't turn around, didn't move, just stood there, fists trembling with rage. "You told him everything. You fucking idiot!"

The man on the bed didn't look up. His voice cracked when he spoke, broken and weak. "I didn't mean to. I didn't mean—"

"You ruined us!" The man by the window spun around, his face blurred, twisted in anger. Alen's breath caught in his throat. He couldn't see the man's face, but he could feel his fury, his hatred, radiating from him like heat from a fire. "You've ruined everything."

Alen wanted to move, wanted to leave, but his body wouldn't listen. His feet were glued to the floor, his chest tight with fear. The air felt like it was crushing him, squeezing the breath out of his lungs.

"I loved you," the man on the bed whispered, his voice barely audible over the weight of the silence. "I didn't mean to…"

The man by the window took a step forward, his blurred face contorting into something monstrous, something *wrong*. "You shouldn't be here."

Alen's heart slammed against his chest, the words echoing through the room, crawling under his skin. He tried to turn, to run, but his feet wouldn't move. He was trapped, frozen in place as the shadows around him seemed to stretch, pulling closer, swallowing the light.

"You shouldn't be here, get the fuck out!" the man said again, his voice darker, angrier. The air was thick, suffocating, pressing against Alen's chest until he couldn't breathe.

Alen woke up with a start, gasping for air. His sheets were soaked with sweat, his body trembling. The room was freezing, colder than it had any right to be, and he felt like something was still there, lurking in the shadows. He sat up, trying to calm his racing heart, but the dream wouldn't let go. It clung to him, wrapping around his mind like a fucking noose.

He glanced at the clock—3:33 a.m. Of course.

Alen rubbed his hands over his face, trying to shake off the cold that had settled deep in his bones. It wasn't just a dream. He could feel it. The house was trying to tell him something. It was in his head now, crawling into his sleep, making it impossible to tell what was real and what wasn't.

He sat there for what felt like hours, staring at the dark corners of the room, half-expecting to see one of those blurred faces watching him. But there was nothing. Just the silence. Just the cold.

By morning, Alen hadn't slept at all. He wandered into the kitchen, exhausted, his hands shaking as he poured himself a cup of coffee. He stared down at the dark liquid, his mind still tangled up in the dream.

Sam strolled in, yawning, his hair sticking up in all directions. He grabbed a mug from the counter, glancing over at Alen. "You look like shit, man. Did you even sleep?"

Alen shook his head, not looking up. "No."

Sam poured himself some coffee, leaning against the counter. "Still having those weird dreams?"

Alen didn't say anything for a second, just stared into his coffee like it held the answer to what the hell was happening to him. "Yeah," he finally muttered. "Still happening."

Sam shrugged, taking a sip of his coffee. "Don't let it get to you, man. It's just a house."

Alen forced a smile, but the pit in his stomach told him otherwise. It wasn't just the house anymore. It was something else. Something darker. And no matter how hard he tried to ignore it, it was digging deeper into him every day.

Sam shrugged, taking a sip of his coffee. "Don't let it get to you, man. It's just a house."

Alen forced a smile, but the pit in his stomach told him otherwise. It wasn't just the house anymore. It was something else. Something darker. And no matter how hard he tried to ignore it, it was digging deeper into him every day.

Chapter 10: Into Town

The house had gotten colder. The supplies were low, and everyone was feeling the weight of staying in a place that seemed to chill right to the bone. Alen stood in the kitchen, staring at the few cans left on the counter, knowing they'd have to make a run into town soon.

"We're running out of everything," Alen said, shaking his head. "If we don't go into town now, we're gonna be stuck eating beans and stale crackers."

Cody, who had been rummaging through the cabinets, straightened up with a scowl. "Yeah, I'm over it. We need real food. Something that doesn't come out of a damn can."

Sarah groaned from the couch, where she was wrapped in a blanket. "Hell yes. I could go for a greasy burger right about now."

Sam walked in, glancing at his phone, his eyebrows pulling together in a slight frown. "Weather's turning to crap. Forecast says there's gonna be a lot of rain later. If we're heading out, we better do it soon before we get stuck on the roads."

Alen glanced out the window, where dark clouds were starting to gather, thick and heavy. "Alright, let's head out now. Get food, stock up, and get back before the storm hits."

The drive into town was quiet. The sky was turning darker with every mile they put behind them, the first few raindrops splattering on the windshield. Sam turned on the wipers, the low squeak of rubber filling the cab of the truck. They pulled into town just as the rain picked up, the streets looking deserted except for a few cars scattered along the curb.

Sam parked the truck outside the diner, its flickering neon sign casting a faint glow over the rain-soaked street. "Let's eat first," Sam said, cutting the engine. "If we're stocking up, we might as well get a decent meal in us first."

"I'm down," Cody said, already halfway out of the truck. "Anything beats another night of canned beans."

They hurried inside, shaking off the rain as they stepped through the door. The diner was mostly empty, just a few people scattered at the counter sipping coffee and talking in low voices. The smell of grease and hot coffee hit them as they slid into a booth near the window.

Cody grabbed the menu, flipping it open eagerly. "I'm ordering the biggest burger they've got. Fries, too. No more canned crap for me."

"I hear that," Sarah said, pulling her hair out of her face as she glanced at the menu. "I want something hot and greasy. And a milkshake. Screw it."

The waitress, an older woman with tired eyes, came over with a pen and pad in hand. "What can I get you folks?"

They rattled off their orders burgers, fries, milkshakes, the works. Once the waitress had walked away, the rain outside had picked up even more, tapping harder against the window.

"We should get supplies quick after this," Sam said, glancing out at the downpour. "I don't want to be stuck driving in this if the roads flood."

Cody raised an eyebrow. "You think it'll get that bad?"

Sam shrugged. "Could. These old roads wash out quick if the storm's bad enough. We should be fine if we get out of here soon."

They had just started digging into their burgers when the door to the diner swung open, letting in a blast of cold air and a guy in a rain-soaked jacket. He walked in slowly, shaking the rain from his jacket as he glanced around the room. Alen didn't recognize him, but something about the way he scanned the room made him uneasy.

The guy spotted their table and walked over, his boots squeaking on the floor as he came to a stop beside them.

"Working on that old house up the road, huh?" he asked, his voice low and rough.

Alen blinked, setting his burger down. "Uh, yeah. How'd you know?"

The man shrugged, his eyes drifting to the window where the rain continued to hammer down. "Word gets around in a town this small. People talk about that house."

Cody looked up from his food, narrowing his eyes. "What's it to you?"

The guy didn't answer right away. He just stood there, his expression hard to read. "Just saying... be careful. That house has a reputation."

Alen frowned. "What do you mean?"

The man's eyes shifted back to Alen, and his voice dropped even lower. "Bad things happen there. Always have. If you're smart, you won't stay there too long."

The air at the table seemed to drop a few degrees. Cody glanced at Sam, then back at the guy. "What kind of 'bad things' are we talking about?"

The man didn't answer. He just gave them one last, lingering look, then turned and walked out into the rain without another word, leaving them sitting there in stunned silence.

For a moment, no one said anything. The rain pounded against the windows, and the sound of the door closing echoed through the nearly empty diner.

"Well, that wasn't creepy at all," Sarah said finally, picking at her fries.

Cody snorted. "What the hell was that about?"

Alen shook his head, his appetite fading a little after the strange encounter, but he forced himself to finish his burger. "I don't know. But let's finish up and grab our supplies. The rain's getting worse."

They ate the rest of their meal, the conversation falling quiet as the sound of rain against the windows grew louder. Even with the warmth of the diner and the smell of hot food filling the air, the uneasy feeling from the man's warning clung to them.

Chapter 11: Trapped by the Storm

The rain was hammering down by the time they climbed back into the truck, loud enough to drown out their voices. Alen was behind the wheel, leaning forward like that would help him see through the downpour, but the windshield wipers weren't doing much. Cody tossed the bag of chips into the backseat and sighed.

"Jesus, it's like driving through a friggin' waterfall."

"No kidding," Sam muttered, pulling on his seatbelt. "These roads better not flood, or we're screwed."

Sarah hugged her jacket tighter, shivering a little. "I don't like this. We should've left sooner."

Alen didn't say anything, just gripped the steering wheel harder. The sky was nearly black, clouds thick and swirling, and the rain was coming down sideways. The trees lining the road were bending, swaying, and snapping in the wind.

The truck crawled forward, the tires sloshing through puddles that were getting bigger by the second. Every time they hit one, the truck jerked a little.

"So, uh... that guy back at the diner," Cody said, leaning forward between the seats. "Think he was serious about the house?"

Sam snorted. "Come on. Some random dude trying to freak us out. Towns like this, they see people like us and think it's funny to mess with us."

Sarah didn't look convinced. "He didn't seem like he was messing with us, though. He looked... off."

"Yeah, well," Sam shot back, "what's he gonna say? 'Welcome to the neighborhood, enjoy your haunted mansion?'"

Alen's grip tightened on the wheel as he jerked the truck around another curve, the road barely visible under all the water. "Can we not do this right now? I'm trying not to get us killed out here."

That shut them up for a minute, everyone sitting in silence while the rain battered the truck, and the wind whipped the trees around like ragdolls. The headlights barely cut through the storm, just enough to see the road in front of them, but not much else.

Then something darted across the road. Alen slammed the brakes, the tires slipping on the slick pavement, the whole truck fishtailing hard. "Shit!"

Cody was thrown forward, grabbing the back of Sam's seat. "What the hell was that?"

"Dunno," Sam said, his voice tight. "Let's just keep moving. I don't care what it was."

Alen sat there for a second, his heart still pounding, knuckles white against the steering wheel. He looked into the rearview mirror, but the rain was coming down so hard it was just a blur. "We're fine. Let's just... get back to the house."

They finally pulled up to Alastar Manor, and it looked worse than when they'd left it. The place stood there in the storm like a shadow, water running down the walls in thick streams. The windows were dark, and the wind was rattling the old shutters hard enough that they might fall off.

"Creepy as hell," Cody muttered, staring up at the house. "Creepier in the rain."

Alen killed the engine, leaning back in his seat for a second before exhaling. "Come on, let's get this stuff inside before we drown."

They all grabbed bags and made a run for it, boots splashing through the puddles already forming in the driveway. By the time they got to the porch, they were soaked to the bone, shivering. The front door creaked as they pushed it open, and the inside wasn't much better—cold as ice, like the house itself had been waiting for them.

Sam dropped his bag on the floor and rubbed his arms. "Why the hell is it so cold in here? Feels colder inside than out there."

"Tell me about it," Sarah grumbled, huddling by the fireplace, fumbling with matches to get the fire going. "I can't feel my fingers."

Alen shook the water off his jacket, dropping it on the floor with a splat. He glanced around. The house felt... different now. Darker. Colder. Something about being back here after that guy's warning didn't sit right with him.

Cody wandered over to the window, rubbing his arms, his breath puffing out in front of him. He peered out at the road, his face tensing. "Uh, guys... I don't think we're going anywhere."

Sam frowned. "What are you talking about?"

"The road," Cody said, not taking his eyes off it. "It's fucking gone. Totally flooded."

Alen came over, staring out the window. Sure enough, the dirt road that led them here was now a small river, water rushing over it. "Shit. We're stuck."

No one said anything for a second. Just the crackle of the fire Sarah finally got going and the pounding rain on the roof.

"Well, that's fucking perfect," Cody muttered, turning away from the window. "Now what? We just wait this shit out?"

Sam sighed, tossing another log on the fire. "What else are we gonna do?"

They all stood there for a second, the weight of it settling in. They were stuck in a house that was too cold, too dark, and now there was no way out until the storm passed. Alen could still hear the guy's voice in his head: *Bad things happen there. Always have.*

The rain hadn't let up at all, just hammering the windows, the wind shaking the whole place. Sarah was huddled by the fire, rubbing her hands together. Cody was pacing, clearly annoyed. "You guys hear that?"

Alen looked over. "Hear what?"

Cody paused, tilting his head. "Like... creaking. Upstairs. Thought it was the wind, but it's been going on for a while."

They all stopped, listening. At first, it was just the storm, the rain pounding against the windows, the fire crackling softly. But then, faintly, there it was a oft creaking, like footsteps, moving slowly across the floor above them.

Chapter 12: Cody's Nightmare

The rain hammered the windows, drowning out almost everything else. Sam stood at the stove, flipping steaks in a cast-iron pan. The sizzle was the only sound competing with the storm outside. Cody leaned against the counter, arms crossed, watching the food cook.

"Feels like the damn house is colder every minute," Cody muttered, rubbing his arms. "We're gonna freeze if this storm keeps up."

"Tell me about it," Sam said, not taking his eyes off the pan. "I swear, this place has no insulation."

Alen was at the table, peeling a few potatoes. "Keep the fire going, and we'll be alright. It's just the storm messing with everything."

Cody glanced at the windows, the shadows of the trees swaying in the gusts. "It's not just the cold. This place feels... I don't know, weird."

Sarah came over, tossing some plates on the table. "Creepy house, creepy weather. What a combination. But hey, dinner's almost ready, so let's just eat before we freak ourselves out."

Finally, they sat down at the table, plates filled with steak, mashed potatoes, and a salad Sarah had thrown together. The room felt too quiet, even with the storm beating against the windows. They ate in silence for a while, each one lost in their own thoughts.

"This is good," Cody said around a mouthful of food, trying to break the tension. "Better than I expected."

Sam grinned. "See? I don't just look good, I cook too."

Sarah laughed. "Modest as always."

Cody chuckled, but it faded quick. He pushed his plate away, suddenly not feeling all that hungry. "So... what's the plan? The road's washed out. We're stuck here. We can't just sit around and wait."

Alen shrugged, wiping his mouth with his sleeve. "We don't really have a choice, do we? Storm's gotta end sometime. Once the road clears, we can leave."

"Yeah, but what if it doesn't clear up right away?" Sarah asked, her voice softer. "You think we're good to stay here for a few days?"

Sam waved a hand. "We'll be fine. It's a house, not a prison. And that guy at the diner? He was just trying to spook us. This isn't some haunted shit."

Cody didn't look convinced. "Yeah, but something feels off, man. I can't explain it. Just... bad vibes all around."

Alen leaned back in his chair, stretching. "You're thinking too much. It's just the storm, and we're all a little tired. Let's just get through the night."

They finished the meal in relative quiet, but the tension lingered. The fire crackled weakly in the corner, throwing flickering shadows across the room, making everything feel colder than it should have. No one wanted to admit it, but the house—hell, the whole night—just felt *wrong*.

Alen was the first to call it a night. "I'm crashing. We'll figure it out in the morning."

"Same here," Sarah said, standing and stretching. "I need sleep. This storm is draining the hell outta me."

Sam gave Cody a nod as he stood up. "You heading up?"

Cody shook his head. "Nah, I'll hang by the fire for a bit. Try to unwind."

Sam shrugged, giving him a small smile. "Alright, man. Don't stay up too late."

One by one, they all retreated to their rooms, leaving Cody alone by the weak fire. He stared into the flames for a while, but his mind was somewhere else—on the storm outside, on the way the house creaked like it was alive, and... on Sam.

He didn't know how long he sat there, thinking, feeling the strange tension in his chest. Eventually, though, the fire started dying out, and the cold finally pushed him to drag himself upstairs.

Cody wasn't asleep for long before he heard it—soft, but clear. A knock at the door.

He blinked, groggy, his mind still fuzzy from sleep. "Yeah? Who is it?"

"Cody?" Sam's voice. Quiet, almost hesitant. "You still awake?"

Cody rubbed his eyes and sat up, the blankets tangled around him. "Yeah, come in."

The door creaked open, and there was Sam, leaning against the doorframe like he was unsure of himself. He stepped into the room slowly, his eyes on Cody. "Hey, man. You got a minute?"

Cody's heart was thudding, though he couldn't explain why. "Uh, yeah. What's up?"

Sam crossed the room and sat down on the edge of the bed, a little closer than usual. His voice was softer now, almost careful. "I, uh... I know how you feel about me."

Cody's breath caught. "What? What do you mean?"

Sam looked down for a second, then back at Cody with a small smile. "I've known for a while. And... I feel the same."

Cody's chest tightened. He didn't know what to say. "You... you do?"

Sam nodded, his voice low. "Yeah. I've wanted you for a long time, Cody."

Before Cody could respond, Sam leaned in, his lips brushing against Cody's. The kiss was soft, slow at first, then more urgent. Cody's mind spun, but all he could think was *this is happening*. His hands found their way to Sam's back, pulling him closer.

They kissed again, deeper this time, and soon clothes were falling to the floor, tangled around their feet. Sam slipped under the blanket with him, his body warm against Cody's.

Cody's breath caught in his throat as Sam pressed against him, hard and solid, his weight pinning him down. But then something shifted. Sam's touch—so soft at first—became rougher, almost painful.

Cody winced, trying to pull back. "Hey, man, slow down. You're being too rough."

Sam's breath was hot, ragged. "You like it, don't you? This is what you wanted."

Cody's pulse raced, but something wasn't right. He tried to push Sam away, but his hands wouldn't move. "Sam, seriously—stop."

But Sam's grip tightened, his hands digging into Cody's skin. "This is what you've been waiting for," Sam whispered, his voice darker now, colder.

Cody opened his eyes—and froze.

It wasn't Sam. It was... something else.

Hovering over him was a grotesque face, twisted and warped. The skin was cracked, bloody, and its eyes were black pits, empty and staring. Its breath came out in harsh, guttural gasps, smelling of rot.

"Don't worry," the thing rasped, its voice deep and broken. "This'll only hurt a lot."

Cody tried to scream, but the thing's weight crushed him, suffocating him. Pain shot through his body, sharp and burning, and he screamed again, thrashing, but it didn't let go.

Just as the pain became unbearable, everything went dark.

Cody bolted upright in bed, gasping for air, his body drenched in sweat. He was shaking, his heart pounding so hard it felt like it might break through his ribs. He looked around the room, but it was just him. No creature, no Sam. Just him, alone in the dark.

But that fear—the panic—it was still there, thick in his chest. He could feel it clinging to him, like it hadn't just been a dream.

It had felt too real.

Chapter 13: Voices Unseen

Cody hadn't been the same since that nightmare. That thing—whatever the hell it was—had left something behind, something crawling under his skin. He could still feel it, like it hadn't let go of him, like it was *waiting*.

He stood in the kitchen with the others, but he wasn't really there. The sound of the rain beating on the windows and the low murmur of their voices faded into the background as his thoughts spun. Every time he closed his eyes, he saw that grotesque face, those hollow, black eyes staring at him.

Sam noticed. "You alright, man? You've been kinda... off all day."

Cody blinked, snapping back to the present. "Yeah, I'm good. Just... tired, I guess."

Sam wasn't buying it. "Nah, you've been in your own head all morning. Still hung up on that dream?"

Cody hesitated, not wanting to admit how much that dream was messing with him. "It wasn't just a dream, dude. It felt... *real*. Like, too real."

Sam leaned against the counter, arms crossed, giving Cody a half-smirk. "It's this house, man. The place gets in your head. You'll feel better once this storm's done, and we can get the hell outta here."

Cody nodded, but he wasn't so sure. The house, the storm... something felt *off*. It had felt off since the second they stepped foot inside.

Later, Cody wandered through the house, trying to clear his head, but it wasn't helping. Sam and Sarah were doing their thing downstairs,

Alen was off fixing something in one of the rooms, and the storm wasn't letting up. The wind kept rattling the windows, making the whole place creak like it was alive.

He stopped in front of the door to his room. It was cracked open, just enough for him to see inside. Just looking at it made his stomach twist. Last night's nightmare was still fresh in his head—the way Sam had turned into that thing, the weight of it pinning him down.

He stared at the door, debating whether or not to go inside, but his feet wouldn't move. The idea of walking back into that room made his chest tighten. His heart picked up speed. *Get a grip,* he thought, trying to shake off the nerves. *It was just a dream.*

Still, he didn't go in.

Then he heard it.

A knock, soft at first, like it came from down the hall. Cody froze, glancing back, his pulse quickening. "Hello?"

No answer.

He waited, but the only sound was the rain hammering on the windows. He almost convinced himself he'd imagined it when the knock came again—this time louder. Closer.

He swallowed hard, scanning the hallway, his breath catching in his throat. "Who's there?" His voice came out shaky, too quiet, even to him.

Silence.

He turned to head back, wanting to get the hell out of that hallway, when he saw something. Just a flicker of movement at the end of the hall, like someone had slipped around the corner. His blood went cold. "Sam? Alen?"

No answer.

Cody stood there, heart thudding in his chest, staring down the hall like the walls were closing in on him. "Fuck this."

He spun around to leave, but that's when he heard it again. A whisper this time, barely a breath.

"Cody…"

His heart jumped into his throat. The voice—it was low, soft, like someone was standing right behind him. He turned around fast, but the hall was empty. Completely still.

The whisper came again, closer this time, sending a shiver straight down his spine. "Cody…"

He backed up, his hands shaking, trying to push the panic down, but it wasn't working. "Who the fuck's messing with me?" he called out, his voice cracking.

The air felt thick, pressing in around him. His chest tightened as he tried to calm down, but it was no use. It felt like someone was breathing down his neck. He could almost feel it.

His eyes darted down the hall. No one there. But that voice—*that fucking voice*—was still in his head.

"Cody…"

That was it. He bolted.

Feet pounding against the floor, he didn't care where he was going, as long as it was away from that voice. He tore down the stairs and skidded into the kitchen, almost slamming into Sam.

"Whoa, dude! What the hell?" Sam jumped back, startled.

Cody leaned against the counter, chest heaving, trying to catch his breath. "I… I don't know."

Sam raised an eyebrow. "You look like you saw a ghost, man. What's going on?"

Cody wiped sweat from his forehead, his hands still shaking. "I thought… I thought I heard something. I don't know, man. Something's off."

Sam studied him for a second, frowning. "You're not making sense. You sure you're alright?"

"I'm not fucking alright," Cody snapped, then immediately regretted it. He ran a hand through his hair, shaking his head. "I'm just... I don't know. I thought I heard someone, and then... there was nothing."

Sam exhaled, stepping back. "Look, we're all feeling weird in here, okay? It's the house, the storm, all of it. It's getting in your head. You're not losing it."

Cody wanted to believe him, but that chill still sat in his gut. He didn't say it out loud, but he knew—*it* was still here. That thing from his dream, or whatever the fuck it was, hadn't left.

And now it was starting to mess with him when he was awake.

Chapter 14: Sarah

Sarah couldn't shake the feeling that this house was screwing with her. She was usually the level-headed one, the one who could roll with the punches. But right now? The house was getting to her, and she fucking hated it.

After dinner, she grabbed the plates, heading into the kitchen. "I'll clean up," she muttered, more to herself than anyone else. Cody and Sam were still talking about the storm, but she didn't care. She just needed to move, to *do* something that wasn't sitting around and stewing in the bad vibes this place was giving off.

The kitchen felt colder, like a draft had slipped in, even though there shouldn't have been one. She rubbed her arms, trying to fight off the chill, and wiped down the counter, her hands moving on autopilot. The wind was howling outside, loud enough to make her flinch every time it slammed into the windows.

This house is bullshit, she thought, scrubbing harder than necessary. She wasn't about to admit it out loud, but this place was creeping her out more than she expected.

And then she heard it.

"Sarah..."

She froze, her hand tightening around the dishcloth. It was faint, like a whisper carried on the wind. Her eyes darted to the hallway, her heart giving a little jump. "Hello?" she called out, her voice shaky. She hated how weak she sounded.

Nothing. Just the wind and the old house settling.

She exhaled, forcing herself to relax. *I'm hearing shit. That's all. Just the storm.* She turned back to the counter, trying to brush it off, but her pulse was still racing.

Then she heard it again.

"Sarah..."

Louder this time. Closer. Her stomach flipped, and she took a step toward the hallway, squinting into the shadows. "Sam? Cody?"

Silence.

Her heart thudded in her chest, and a cold sweat broke out along her skin. She walked to the edge of the hallway, the dim light from the kitchen barely cutting through the shadows. "Guys, this isn't funny."

Still nothing.

She rubbed her arms, suddenly aware of how quiet the house had gotten. Even the wind outside seemed muffled, like the whole place was holding its breath. She backed up, her eyes flicking down the long hallway. Every door looked darker, more menacing. The walls felt like they were closing in on her.

"Get a grip," she muttered to herself, shaking her head. But the dread was already creeping in, tightening around her chest.

The floorboards creaked behind her.

She spun around, her heart leaping into her throat. But there was no one there. Just the empty kitchen, and the shadows that seemed to be stretching further and further down the hall.

Then, from the corner of her eye, she saw it.

A figure. Faint, standing at the end of the hallway.

Her breath caught, and her skin prickled with cold. "Cody?" she called, her voice barely a whisper now.

The figure didn't move. Didn't blink. Just stood there, staring at her from the shadows.

Her pulse was pounding now, her hands shaking. She took a hesitant step forward. "Sam?"

No response.

Her gut twisted, every nerve in her body screaming at her to turn around and *run*. But her feet wouldn't move. The figure seemed to flicker, like it wasn't really there, and then—it was gone.

Vanished. Like smoke.

"What the fuck," she whispered, taking a shaky step back. She turned, ready to get the hell out of the hallway, when she heard it again.

"Sarah..."

Right in her ear.

She yelped, spinning around so fast she almost tripped over her own feet. Her breath came in short, panicked bursts, her eyes darting around the hallway, but there was nothing. Just that eerie, suffocating silence.

Her legs finally got the message, and she bolted toward the living room. Her feet hit the floor hard, her heart hammering in her chest. She didn't stop until she burst into the room, almost crashing into Sam.

"Whoa, whoa!" Sam said, catching her by the arms. "Sarah, what the hell?"

She was panting, trying to catch her breath, but the words wouldn't come out. She could still hear the whisper in her head, like it was crawling through her mind.

Cody stood up, his eyes wide. "Sarah? What happened?"

"I... I heard something," she managed to say, her voice shaky. "Someone was calling my name."

Sam frowned, exchanging a look with Cody. "Calling you? Who?"

"I don't know!" she snapped, running a hand through her hair, her hands still trembling. "I thought it was you guys, but... there was something else. At the end of the hallway. It kept calling me."

Cody's face went pale. "You... saw something?"

She nodded, feeling the weight of their eyes on her, but she didn't care. "Yeah. I saw it. It was standing there. Just... staring."

The room went dead quiet. The fire crackled weakly, the storm still pounding outside, but everything felt still. Too still.

Sam stepped back, rubbing his face. "Fuck, man. This place is getting to all of us."

Cody swallowed, his eyes darting to the hallway. "You're not the only one hearing shit. This house... I don't know, man. Something's fucked up."

Sarah felt it then, that deep, gnawing dread settling in her gut. Whatever it was—whatever had called her name—it wasn't done with them. It was just getting started.

Chapter 15: Sam

Sam had hit his limit. Between the storm, Cody freaking out, and Sarah acting all weird, he needed a break. The house was doing a number on them, and even though he tried to stay chill, the shit was getting to him too. He rubbed his neck, his muscles aching from the stress, and figured a hot shower might help shake off the bad vibes clinging to him.

Upstairs, the bathroom was cold as hell. He shivered, peeling off his shirt and tossing it onto the floor. The mirror caught a glimpse of him—tall, built solid, with broad shoulders and faint scars from old football injuries still showing through his tan skin. His chest and abs were defined, but right now, he wasn't feeling strong at all.

All he wanted was the heat to hit him, the steam to fog up the room, and maybe drown out the noise in his head. *You're just tired,* he told himself, stripping down to nothing, his body tightening against the chill.

He stepped into the shower and twisted the knob, waiting for the water to heat up. The first blast was cold as shit, making him jump back with a muttered curse. *Fucking house,* he thought, running a hand over his face. The pipes groaned, but finally, the water warmed up, and the heat hit his back like a welcome blanket.

"Thank fuck," he muttered, closing his eyes, letting the water run over his head, down his chest. It felt good. The tension in his muscles started to ease up, the heat working its way through his body. He stood there, letting it all wash away.

His mind drifted to Sarah and Cody, how weird they'd been acting all night. Whispering, seeing shadows, hearing shit. The house was getting to them for sure, and it was trying to get to him too. But no way he'd let it. He wasn't about to lose his cool like Cody. He just needed to focus, keep his head on straight, and—

CREAK.

Sam froze.

His eyes snapped open, the hot water still pouring over him, but something had shifted in the room. He could've sworn he'd heard something. Maybe the old pipes. Or maybe... not.

Don't do this, he told himself, rubbing water out of his eyes. He stood there for a second, listening, trying to calm his racing heart. The house creaked again, but it could've been the wind. Could've been anything. But it was enough to make the hairs on the back of his neck stand up.

He turned, his body tense, scanning the shower through the haze of steam. The glass was fogged up, and outside the shower, the rest of the room was a blur. He stared hard, squinting through the glass, waiting for something to move.

Nothing.

He ran a hand through his wet hair, sighing, trying to shake the tension creeping back into his chest. *You're being paranoid, man.* The others were just putting shit in his head, making him think something was there when it wasn't. He grabbed the soap, ready to finish up and get the hell out.

But then—*thud.*

Sam's breath caught. This time, the noise was louder. Closer. His heart thumped hard against his ribs. He stood still, eyes wide, his ears straining to hear. The bathroom was dead quiet, except for the water trickling down the drain, and the eerie feeling that something was off.

It's just the house, he told himself, his stomach flipping. *Just this old-ass house.*

But it didn't feel right.

He turned off the water, the sudden silence almost too loud, and stepped out of the shower. His feet hit the cold tiles, and he wrapped a towel around his waist, wiping steam off his face with the edge of it. The room was thick with fog, the mirror completely fogged over. He stared at it for a second, his breath shallow, his pulse still racing.

And that's when he saw it.

A handprint.

Right in the middle of the fogged mirror. Wet, fresh, like someone had just pressed their palm against it and dragged it down.

Sam's stomach dropped. His throat went dry. *What the fuck?*

"Cody? Sarah?" His voice came out too loud, bouncing off the tiles, but no one answered. The air felt heavier now, thick, like the room had closed in around him.

His hands shook as he wiped a streak through the fogged mirror, clearing just enough space to see his reflection.

But something wasn't right.

He blinked, staring at himself. Or... was it even him? His reflection didn't move. It just stood there, still, like a picture, staring back at him.

Sam stepped back, heart hammering, a cold sweat breaking out across his skin. The reflection *should* have moved with him. But it didn't. It stayed put, grinning.

"What the hell..."

The light flickered, the room dimming for a split second, and when it came back on, his reflection grinned wider, teeth sharp, eyes dark—too dark.

Sam stumbled back, the towel slipping from his waist. "No, no, no," he whispered, his body cold now, trembling. He spun around, half-expecting someone—*something*—to be there, but the room was empty.

The light flickered again, and he swore the walls were closing in. The air was so thick he could barely breathe, like the steam had turned into something else—something alive.

A cold gust brushed against his back, and Sam's breath hitched. He turned, slowly, his eyes darting around the fogged-up room, but there was no one. Just the steam, the thick air, the suffocating silence.

Then the shower turned on again.

But this time, the water wasn't hot. It was ice cold, the spray hitting the tiles like a sudden burst of winter air.

Sam's pulse shot up, his body frozen with fear, his skin prickling. His instincts screamed at him to run, to get the hell out, but his legs wouldn't move. The door was closed—he didn't remember closing it—and the room felt smaller, like it was pressing in on him.

And then... the shower curtain moved. Just a little, but enough.

Something's in here with me.

Sam's breath came in short, panicked gasps as he forced his feet to move, slipping on the wet tiles. He yanked the door open, his heart racing, and stumbled into the hallway, cold air hitting his bare skin. The bathroom door slammed shut behind him, rattling in its frame, and he jumped, crashing into the opposite wall.

He stood there, chest heaving, water dripping off him, the towel barely hanging on. For a long moment, he didn't move, just stared at the door, every nerve in his body screaming that something was still watching him.

Chapter 16: Alen

Alen stood there staring at the wall, trying to fight off the frustration bubbling up inside him. He'd been working on the same damn crack for an hour, and no matter what he did, it just kept coming back. Wider, darker, like the house was laughing at him.

"Are you fucking kidding me?" he muttered, slamming the trowel down on the floor. His hands were shaking, and he wiped them on his jeans, but it didn't help. He was tired. Tired of the house, tired of the storm, tired of all the weird shit that kept happening around them.

He took a deep breath, trying to calm down. "Come on, man, it's just an old house. You're just tired. It's nothing."

But it wasn't nothing. He could feel it in his gut. The whole place felt... off. Like it was pushing back, like it didn't *want* to be fixed.

The rain kept pounding against the windows, the wind howling outside, and the cold air crept in through the cracks, making the whole place feel even emptier than it was. He tried to shrug it off, but the feeling wouldn't go away. Something was wrong here, and he couldn't keep pretending it wasn't.

He looked at the wall again, his stomach twisting. The crack had spread. He hadn't even touched it, and it was worse than before. Darker, deeper, like it was alive.

Nope. Fuck that.

Alen turned, grabbing his stuff, ready to get the hell out of there and leave the crack for another day. He was done. He was done with all of it.

"Alen..."

He froze. His blood went cold, and his heart jumped into his throat. The voice was soft, barely more than a whisper, but he heard it. Clear as day.

"Alen..."

It came again. Closer this time. He whipped around, eyes wide, but there was no one. Just the shadows at the end of the hallway, the flickering light making them stretch and twist.

His chest tightened, and he swallowed hard, trying to push down the rising panic. *You're hearing things,* he told himself. *You're just hearing things. It's the storm. It's all in your head.*

But it didn't feel like it was in his head.

He backed up, his heart pounding in his chest, the hair on his arms standing on end. He could feel something. Watching him. Waiting.

"Who's there?" His voice cracked, sounding way less confident than he wanted. Silence answered back, but it wasn't the comforting kind of silence. It was thick, heavy, like the air itself was holding its breath.

He glanced down the hallway again, squinting into the dark. *Come on, man, get a grip. It's nothing.* He started to turn, to get the hell out of there, but then he heard it again. Louder this time.

"Alen..."

His stomach dropped. That voice—it wasn't just random. It was familiar. Too familiar.

His breath caught in his throat, and for a split second, he couldn't move. Couldn't think. His mind was spinning, his heart racing.

No. No way. It can't be her.

But he knew. Deep down, he fucking knew.

He turned slowly, his pulse thudding in his ears. The shadows at the end of the hallway seemed to shift, like something was moving just out of sight. His skin prickled. Sweat beaded on the back of his neck.

"Alen, why did you leave me?"

The voice hit him like a punch to the gut. He stumbled back, his legs shaky, his breath coming in sharp bursts. "No, no, no, this isn't happening." His voice was barely a whisper now, trembling as much as his hands.

His back hit the wall, and he wiped his palms on his jeans, his chest heaving. "This isn't real. You're not real."

But the voice didn't stop.

"Why did you leave me, Alen?"

The shadows moved again, and this time, he saw it. A figure. Standing just at the edge of the dark, barely visible, but enough to send a wave of cold fear crashing through him.

He knew that shape. He knew it like a bad dream that wouldn't let go.

"You left me," the voice whispered, soft but full of blame. Full of hurt.

Alen's stomach twisted, his throat closing up. *No. This can't be happening.* He backed up, his feet slipping on the hardwood floor. His pulse was racing so hard, he thought his heart might just give out.

He blinked, and the figure was closer. Her face was clearer now. Dark, hollow eyes. Skin pale and twisted, like she'd been pulled from the earth.

"Why did you leave me?"

Alen shook his head, his hands trembling at his sides. "I didn't mean to. I didn't..." His voice broke, cracking under the weight of it all. He couldn't breathe. He couldn't fucking breathe.

"You left me, Alen."

The words echoed around him, bouncing off the walls, filling the air until all he could hear was her voice. The hallway stretched out in front of him, twisting and warping, the shadows crawling up the walls like they were alive.

"I didn't mean to!" he yelled, his chest heaving. "I didn't fucking mean to!"

The figure was right in front of him now, her eyes locked on his, hollow and endless. "You left me, Alen," she whispered, her voice like a knife to his chest.

"I'm sorry," he whispered, barely able to get the words out. "I'm so fucking sorry."

The walls around him seemed to shift, closing in, the crack in the wall spreading, widening, like the house itself was swallowing him whole. His vision blurred, his legs threatening to give out.

"I'm sorry," he whispered again, but the words felt useless. Empty.

The figure didn't move. Didn't speak. She just stood there, her dark eyes staring through him, her presence cold and suffocating. The air felt heavy, pressing down on him, making it harder to breathe.

The hallway around him stretched, the shadows swallowing everything, and Alen knew—there was no way out.

Chapter 17: A House That Watches

The fire flickered weakly in the hearth, barely giving off any heat. It crackled and popped, but the room still felt cold, like something had sucked the warmth out of it. The shadows on the walls stretched long, creeping into the corners, and the air was thick—heavy with unspoken fear.

Cody sat hunched forward, elbows resting on his knees, staring at the floor like it might give him answers. His hands were shaking, and he couldn't stop bouncing his leg. He needed to talk, to get it out. But the words were caught in his throat.

"Fuck," Cody muttered under his breath, finally breaking the silence. "Alright, fine. I'm just gonna say it." He glanced up at the others—Alen, Sarah, Sam—all sitting there, waiting. "I had a dream. But it wasn't a fucking dream, man. It felt... real. Too real."

Alen leaned forward, his brow furrowed. "What happened?"

Cody rubbed his face, his breath shaky. "It was you, Sam. You came to my room. Knocked real soft, like you didn't want to wake anyone. I was half asleep, so I didn't think much of it. I said, 'Yeah, come in.' And you did. You came in, shut the door behind you, and sat on my bed."

Sam frowned. "What?"

"Yeah," Cody's voice was low, rough. "You sat there, real quiet, and we started talking. But it wasn't normal, man. You said... you said you knew how I felt about you." His voice caught, and he looked down, rubbing the back of his neck. "I didn't know what to say, but you—you said you felt the same."

Sam blinked, his voice soft. "Cody... I never—"

"I know!" Cody snapped, his voice cracking. "I fucking know, alright? But it felt so real. You kissed me, man. And I thought... I thought this was happening. We kissed, and it was... it was good. But then... then everything changed."

Alen could see the fear creeping into Cody's eyes, the way his hands started trembling again.

Cody swallowed hard, his voice a little more ragged now. "At first, it was soft, gentle. But then you—no, not you—*it* started getting rough. You grabbed me too hard. Your hands—fuck, they hurt. I told you to stop, but you didn't. You just kept saying, 'This is what you wanted, right?' But it wasn't your voice anymore. It was darker. Rougher."

The room was dead silent. The fire popped again, but it sounded far away.

Cody's eyes flicked up, locking onto Sam. "I opened my eyes, and it wasn't you. It wasn't you at all. There was this... this fucking thing. Its face was twisted, skin all cracked, eyes black as hell. It grinned at me, like it knew I couldn't do shit. It pinned me down, Sam. I couldn't fucking breathe. I couldn't move. And then it leaned in close, and it whispered in my ear, 'This'll only hurt a lot.'"

Sam sat back, his face pale, his leg bouncing nervously.

"I tried to scream, but nothing came out," Cody's voice cracked. "It was crushing me, man. I thought I was gonna die. Then everything went dark, like it swallowed me whole. I woke up drenched in sweat, shaking, my heart pounding like it was about to explode. But even when I woke up... I felt like it was still there. Like it left something behind."

Alen's stomach twisted. Cody wasn't one to get freaked out easily, but right now, he looked like he was barely holding it together.

Cody rubbed his face again, trying to steady his breath. "It wasn't just a fucking nightmare, Alen. I know it wasn't. That thing... it felt *real*."

The room was tense, the kind of silence that presses on your chest, makes you feel like you're suffocating. No one knew what to say. The fire flickered, casting long shadows across the walls, but it didn't warm the room at all.

Alen shifted in his seat, his own heart pounding. He'd been trying to ignore what had happened to him, to push it down, but he couldn't anymore. Cody wasn't the only one.

"I had a dream, too," Alen said, his voice low. "But it wasn't a dream. Not really."

Cody looked up, his eyes still wide, haunted. "You too?"

Alen nodded, rubbing his hands together, trying to warm them up. "Yeah. I didn't even want to sleep last night. I knew something was waiting for me if I did. But eventually, I drifted off, and... fuck, man. The house was in my head. Like it was alive. It was suffocating me."

Sarah shifted uncomfortably, watching him carefully.

"I was in the hallway," Alen continued, his voice rough. "But it wasn't normal. It stretched out in front of me, too long, too narrow, like it was pulling me in. The air was so cold, it burned. I couldn't breathe, but I couldn't stop walking, either. My legs felt like they were wading through water. Slow, heavy."

Alen's hands tightened into fists. "There were voices, too. Low, muffled, angry. I couldn't make out what they were saying, but I could feel the hate. It was thick, suffocating, like it was pressing down on me."

Cody's breath hitched. "Jesus..."

Alen shook his head, his chest tight. "I didn't want to go through that door, but I didn't have a choice. My feet kept dragging me toward it. I pushed it open, and the cold hit me like a punch in the gut. The room was wrong. It looked normal at first—bed made, curtains swaying—but the air was... alive. Something dark was crawling over my skin, making my heart race."

Sarah's eyes were wide now, her face pale.

"There were two men," Alen continued, his voice trembling. "One standing by the window, the other sitting on the bed. They didn't see me. It was like I wasn't even there. But the tension between them... it was thick, choking the air. The guy by the window, he was furious. Shaking with rage. His fists were clenched, and he turned to the other one and said, 'You fucking ruined us. You told him everything.'"

Alen's breath caught in his throat, the memory wrapping around him like a noose. "The guy on the bed... he was broken, man. Head in his hands, shoulders shaking. He said, 'I didn't mean to.' His voice was cracked, weak. And then the other guy... he turned. I couldn't see his face, but I could feel the hate. It was like a fucking fire. He said, 'You shouldn't be here. Get the fuck out.' But he wasn't talking to the guy on the bed. He was talking to me."

Cody's face went pale. "What?"

"Yeah," Alen muttered. "His words were crawling under my skin. The air got heavier, and I couldn't move. The shadows stretched, swallowing the light, pulling closer. And then... I woke up. Gasping for air, drenched in sweat. My heart was pounding so hard, I thought I was gonna die. And even then... I felt like something was still in the room with me. Like it hadn't let go."

The fire crackled softly, but it felt miles away. Alen could see it in their faces—they were all feeling it. The house wasn't just a house. It was alive. And it was pushing its way into their heads, their nightmares.

Sarah sat there, her arms wrapped around her knees, her face tight. She'd been quiet for too long, and now, Alen could see she was shaking, trying to hold something back.

"Sarah?" Alen said softly. "What happened?"

Sarah blinked, her eyes glassy, like she was somewhere else for a moment. Then she let out a breath, her voice shaky. "You really wanna know?"

Cody nodded, eyes wide. "Yeah, we need to know."

Sarah swallowed hard, her fingers gripping her arms. "Last night, after dinner, I stayed back to clean up. The storm was loud as hell, and I figured it was just fucking with my head. I kept telling myself it was just the wind. Just the rain. But then... I started hearing my name."

Alen frowned. "Your name?"

"Yeah," she muttered, her voice barely above a whisper. "It was soft at first, like someone whispering it from another room. I ignored it. Figured it was just the house playing tricks on me. But it got louder. Closer. Like someone was standing right behind me, saying my name over and over."

Cody shifted uncomfortably. "Fuck."

Sarah nodded, her breath uneven. "I called out, thought maybe it was one of you fucking with me. But no one answered. The air got cold—real cold. Like ice-cold. And then I turned toward the hallway, and that's when I saw it."

Cody's breath caught. "Saw what?"

"A figure," Sarah's voice shook. "At the end of the hallway. It wasn't clear, just a shadow, standing there. Watching me. I couldn't see its face, but I knew it was staring right at me. I tried to move, but my legs wouldn't fucking move. I was frozen. I could feel it—this cold crawling up my spine, like it was daring me to get closer, but I couldn't. I just... stood there."

Sam leaned forward, his face tight. "What did it do?"

"Nothing," Sarah breathed. "It just stood there, watching. Then, after what felt like forever, it was gone. Just... fucking gone. Like it had never been there. I ran out of there so fast, I nearly knocked into Sam. I didn't say anything because... what the fuck was I supposed to say? That I saw a ghost? No one was gonna believe me."

Cody ran a hand through his hair, his hands trembling. "Shit, Sarah..."

She didn't respond, just hugged her knees tighter, staring into the fire, her breath shaky.

Alen turned to Sam, who had been sitting there quietly, his jaw clenched, his leg bouncing like he was holding something back.

"Sam?" Alen asked softly. "What about you?"

Sam rubbed the back of his neck, his voice tight. "Yeah. Something happened. In the shower."

Cody frowned. "When?"

"Earlier today," Sam muttered. "I was in the shower, trying to clear my head, you know? Hot water, steam. I figured it'd help, but... fuck. I started hearing things."

Sarah leaned forward. "What kind of things?"

Sam's jaw tightened. "Footsteps. Heavy, slow, like someone was walking outside the bathroom door. At first, I thought it was just the pipes or something, but it got louder. I called out—thought maybe one of you was messing with me—but no one answered. And then... the door opened."

Cody's face paled. "What?"

"Yeah," Sam's voice was rough. "The fucking door. It opened, just a crack, real slow, like someone was pushing it from the other side. I didn't see anyone, but it felt like... like something was waiting for me to step out. I wiped the mirror, you know, just to see if anyone was there, and that's when I saw it."

"Saw what?" Alen's voice was tight.

"A handprint," Sam whispered. "Right in the middle of the fogged mirror. Wet, fresh, like someone had pressed their palm against it and dragged it down."

Sarah's breath hitched.

Sam's hands shook as he rubbed them together. "My stomach dropped. My throat went dry. I called out, but no one answered. The air felt heavier, thick, like the room was closing in. I wiped the mirror again, and... fuck, man, my reflection didn't move."

Alen frowned. "What do you mean?"

Sam looked up, his eyes wide with fear. "It didn't move. I wiped the mirror, but when I stepped back, my reflection stayed put. It just stood there, staring at me, grinning."

The room was dead silent.

Sam's voice cracked. "And then it grinned wider. Its teeth were sharp. Its eyes were black—too fucking black. I panicked, spun around, thinking someone was behind me, but there was no one there. The light flickered, and I swear to God, the walls were closing in."

Cody's hands clenched into fists. "Jesus, Sam..."

"I tried to move, but I couldn't," Sam whispered. "The air was thick, like it was alive. Then the shower turned back on—ice cold. The spray hit the tiles like a burst of winter, but I hadn't touched anything. The door was closed. I didn't remember closing it."

Sam ran a hand through his hair, his breath shaky. "And then... the shower curtain moved. Just a little. But enough for me to know something was in there with me. I ran. Didn't even grab my towel. I just bolted out of the room, water dripping off me. The bathroom door slammed behind me, hard. I stood in the hallway, dripping wet, cold as hell, just staring at that door. Whatever's in there... it's still there. I could feel it."

The fire flickered, casting long shadows across the room, but it wasn't enough to chase away the dark.

Cody's voice was barely a whisper. "We're not alone here, are we?"

Alen shook his head, his heart pounding. "No. We're not."

Another creak echoed from upstairs, louder this time, like footsteps making their way toward them.

Chapter 18: House of Shadows

The fire barely flickered anymore. The flames were weak, struggling against the freezing air that had crept in like it belonged there. Cody couldn't stop pacing. His boots thudded against the floor, each step harder than the last, fists clenched so tight his knuckles were white.

"Can't fucking sit here," Cody muttered, more to himself than anyone else. "We can't just sit here and wait to get fucked by this house."

Sarah was curled up on the couch, arms tight around her knees. She shot him a look, voice sharp. "Where the hell are we gonna go, Cody? You looked outside lately? We can't even see the fucking driveway."

Cody stopped, turned to her, his face tight. "Better than sitting here like goddamn bait, waiting for it to come for us."

Alen leaned against the wall, arms crossed. He didn't say much, but his eyes kept darting to the door, like maybe if he stared at it long enough, an escape route would magically appear. But there wasn't shit outside but a storm that felt like it wanted to swallow them whole.

"We can't just run out there," Sam said from the armchair, tapping his fingers against the wood, like it'd keep his nerves from boiling over. "That's suicide. You'll be dead in minutes. Storm'll drown you."

Cody snorted, pacing again. "So we sit here and wait? That's your plan? Just sit here like dumbasses until this thing decides to tear us apart?"

Alen could feel the house pushing in on them. It wasn't even subtle anymore. It wasn't just a house; it was alive. He could feel the walls watching, pressing in, squeezing tighter. The silence wasn't normal. It was like the house was listening, feeding off their fear.

"We need to try the phones again," Alen said, his voice sounding distant, even to himself. "Check if maybe the storm's clearing up."

Cody pulled his phone out, already shaking his head. "Ain't nothing working. This shit's dead." He held up the phone, the screen completely black. No bars, no Wi-Fi, nothing.

Sarah fumbled with hers, hands shaking as she stared down at the screen. "Fuck." She sighed, throwing the phone back into her lap. "It's dead. It's all dead."

Sam took out his own phone, scowling at the empty signal bar. "Yeah, figures. No service. No Wi-Fi. It's like the house is blocking it or some shit."

Alen pulled out his phone, and his heart sank. No bars. No signal. Nothing. It was like the house had cut them off from the rest of the world, leaving them to fend for themselves. They were well and truly alone.

"Fuck," he muttered, running a hand over his face.

Sarah hugged her knees tighter, her voice shaking. "We're on our own. There's no way out."

Cody stuffed his phone back in his pocket, jaw tight. "Then we gotta try the front door again. I'm not just sitting here."

"Try what?" Sam shot back. "You think the storm's gonna let us out now? It's worse out there."

"Better than sitting here waiting for this fucking house to eat us alive," Cody snapped.

Alen shook his head, feeling the tension rising between them. "Cody, the door—"

"I don't give a shit about the door," Cody snapped, marching over to it. "We're getting out of here."

Cody grabbed the handle and yanked. Nothing. He yanked again, harder this time. The door didn't move, didn't budge an inch.

"What the fuck?" Cody muttered, pulling harder.

Sam stood up and shoved Cody aside. "Move." He grabbed the handle, pulled, put his weight into it. Nothing. The door stayed shut. "Shit."

Cody slammed his fist into the door, breathing hard. "This can't be fucking happening."

Sarah backed up, her eyes wide, hands shaking. "It's the house. It—it doesn't want us to leave."

Cody whirled around, his voice rising. "What the fuck do you mean, 'the house doesn't want us to leave'?"

Sam slammed his shoulder into the door again, then cursed under his breath. "She's right, man. It's like it's locked up tight from the inside."

Cody's breath came in fast, ragged bursts, his eyes wild. "You're telling me this fucking house has us trapped?"

Before anyone could answer, there was a loud crack from upstairs. Something heavy, dragging across the floor.

Everyone froze.

Cody's eyes shot up to the ceiling. "What the fuck was that?"

Another crack, this one louder, closer. The fire flickered, shadows dancing along the walls, stretching into the corners.

"It's moving," Sarah whispered, backing away from the door, her face pale. "It's coming."

Alen's pulse quickened, his heart thudding in his chest. The air was thick now, suffocating. It felt like the house was breathing around them, waiting for something to snap.

"We're not going up there," Cody muttered, shaking his head.

"No fucking way," Sam agreed, eyes fixed on the ceiling.

Another thud. Footsteps, slow, deliberate, dragging something behind them. The sound of it made the floorboards groan like they couldn't handle the weight.

"It's coming for us," Sarah whispered, her voice barely audible.

The fire sputtered out, the room plunging into near darkness. Only the storm outside lit up the place, flashes of lightning casting weird, jagged shadows over the walls.

And then the door slammed shut. Hard.

Cody jumped, swearing under his breath. "Fuck this."

Alen felt his pulse race, panic clawing at him. The house was shifting again, and whatever was upstairs was moving closer, step by step. The air felt too thick to breathe, like the house was pressing down on them, tightening around their chests.

Another crash echoed from above, like something heavy had been thrown against the wall. Footsteps followed, each one getting louder, heavier.

Sam grabbed Alen by the arm, his voice tight with fear. "We need to move. Now."

Alen nodded, snapping out of it. "Back room. Now."

They sprinted down the hallway, shoes pounding against the wood floor. Every door they passed felt like it was hiding something, like something was lurking behind it, waiting for them to get close. Alen's breath came in ragged gasps as they slammed into the back room, locking the door behind them.

Cody leaned against the wall, panting hard, his whole body trembling. "This house... it's fucking alive."

Sarah was curled up in the corner, arms around herself, shaking. "It wants us dead. It wants us all dead."

"How?" Sam snapped, pacing the room, his hands clenched into fists. "We can't go out the front, the windows are sealed shut, and whatever the hell that is upstairs isn't just gonna let us walk out."

Alen leaned against the wall, chest heaving. His mind raced, trying to figure out what the fuck to do. The house wasn't just some haunted place—it was something *alive*, something that wanted them scared. And it was working.

And then, from the corner of the room, there was a soft creak.

They all froze.

Something was in there with them.

The air turned cold. Too cold. Alen's breath caught in his throat, his chest tightening. Whatever was in that room with them, it wasn't friendly.

"Alen," Sarah whispered, her voice shaking. "What do we do?"

Alen didn't answer. He didn't know.

Chapter 19: Fractures

The fire barely flickered now, shadows crawling across the walls like they had a life of their own. Cody leaned against the back of the couch, arms crossed tight over his chest, his foot tapping against the wooden floor. His eyes darted toward the door for the hundredth time, as if hoping it would magically fly open and let them escape this nightmare.

Sam sat on the arm of a chair, staring into the dying flames, his eyes glassy, like he wasn't really there. Alen watched him from the other side of the room, arms crossed, trying to shake the feeling that something was... off. Sam had been weird for a while now, but lately, it was like he wasn't *Sam* anymore. Something had changed.

Sarah shifted uncomfortably on the couch, pulling her legs closer to her chest. The room was colder than it should have been, the kind of cold that seeped into your bones, made you shiver no matter how close you were to the fire.

"I'm telling you, we need to try the door again," Cody said, his voice tight. "We can't just fucking sit here."

Sarah's voice was barely above a whisper. "You saw what happened when we tried before. It's not opening."

"So what, we just wait here? For what? To get torn apart?" Cody's voice rose, frustration bleeding through. "Fuck that."

Sam's eyes flicked up from the fire, slowly, like it took effort just to move. His voice was low, almost lazy. "Cody, relax. We're not gonna get torn apart." He gave a small, strange smile. "Not yet, anyway."

Alen frowned, that uneasy feeling growing in his gut. The way Sam had said it—like he *knew* something they didn't. Like he was in on a joke no one else understood.

"What the hell's that supposed to mean?" Cody snapped, turning to Sam. His face was tense, fists clenched at his sides. "You wanna explain that?"

Sam's smile widened, just a little. "I'm saying, you're freaking out over nothing, man. The house—" He paused, his eyes drifting to Cody in a way that made Alen's skin crawl. "It just needs time."

"Time?" Sarah's voice cracked. "What the fuck are you talking about, Sam? We don't have time. You've been acting... weird. Since this morning. Like you know something we don't."

Sam shrugged, eyes still locked on Cody, like he hadn't even heard her. "I'm just saying... we're not alone in here." His voice dropped lower, almost a whisper. "We're never alone."

A chill ran up Alen's spine. He exchanged a look with Sarah, who had gone pale, her hands tightening around her knees. Cody just scoffed, shaking his head.

"Man, what the fuck are you on about?" Cody said, taking a step toward Sam, his voice rising. "You're talkin' like you *know* this place. Like you're part of it or something."

Sam's smile didn't fade. In fact, it grew—just a little—like he was *enjoying* this. "Maybe I do."

Alen's stomach flipped. Something wasn't right. The way Sam was looking at Cody—it was like... hunger. His eyes, dark and glassy, flickered over Cody's face, down his body. Alen shifted uncomfortably, but he couldn't shake the sense that something dangerous was crawling under Sam's skin.

Cody stopped, his eyebrows drawn together, confused. "What the fuck is going on with you?"

Sam stood up slowly, his movements deliberate, like a predator rising from its crouch. He took a step closer to Cody, close enough that Alen could see Cody tense up.

"I've always liked you, Cody," Sam said softly, his voice barely a murmur. "You know that, don't you?"

Cody blinked, stepping back, confused. "What the hell are you talking about?"

Sam's eyes didn't leave him, his voice dropping lower. "I've wanted you... for a long time." He took another step, closing the gap between them. "You've always felt it, haven't you?"

Cody's breath hitched, and Alen could see the panic starting to rise in his eyes. "Sam, stop fuckin' around."

Sam's hand reached out, brushing Cody's arm, slow, almost tender. "You don't have to fight it anymore."

Cody flinched, jerking his arm away. "Sam—what the hell, man?"

Alen moved toward them, heart racing, that creeping feeling crawling up his spine. This wasn't Sam. It couldn't be. Sam wasn't like this. He wasn't...

"You belong to me," Sam whispered, his voice soft but dripping with something dark, something possessive. His eyes locked onto Cody's, and for a split second, Alen thought he saw something *shift* in them—like the darkness behind his pupils was... alive.

"Back the fuck off!" Cody shoved Sam, hard, and Sam stumbled back, but that smile—twisted, wrong—never left his face. He looked like he was *enjoying* this.

"Relax, Cody," Sam said, his voice low, steady. "You don't have to be scared. It's just us now."

Cody's eyes were wide, his breath coming fast, and Alen could see the fear building in his chest. "What the fuck are you saying? What the fuck's wrong with you, man?"

Sam tilted his head, eyes narrowing slightly, and that smile—*that fucking smile*—stayed frozen on his lips. "You don't get it yet, do you?" His voice dropped lower, darker. "I'm not going anywhere."

Alen stepped between them, his hands up, heart pounding in his chest. "Sam, back off. You're freaking him out."

Sam's eyes flicked to Alen, and for a moment, something *sharp* flashed behind them. "Freaking him out?" he repeated, voice laced with sarcasm. "We're all freaked out, aren't we? But Cody... Cody's special."

Alen's jaw tightened. "Sam, enough."

But Sam just smiled again, his head tilting slightly as his eyes dragged over Cody's body in a way that made Alen's stomach churn. It was like watching a predator sizing up its prey.

"He's not special, Sam," Alen said, his voice steady, though his hands were shaking. "You're losing it. Whatever this house is doing to you, you gotta snap out of it."

Sam let out a low laugh, a sound that sent a shiver down Alen's spine. "Snap out of it?" His voice was mocking, cold. "I'm exactly where I need to be. *He's* the one that doesn't get it."

Alen's breath caught in his throat. Sam wasn't himself. This wasn't Sam. It was... something else. Something darker.

"You don't get to tell me what to do anymore," Sam muttered, stepping closer to Alen, his eyes burning with something... *dangerous*. "None of you do."

And just like that, Alen knew. This wasn't Sam anymore. It was something *wearing* him.

Alen swallowed hard, his voice tight. "Sam, whatever's inside you, you gotta fight it."

But Sam—William—just smiled again. "Why would I want to fight it?"

And then he lunged.

Before Alen could react, Sam shoved him aside, slamming him against the wall. The breath left Alen's lungs in a sharp gasp as his back hit the wood with a sickening crack. Sam was on Cody in an instant, grabbing him by the arms, shoving him against the couch with a force that didn't belong to Sam's body.

"You're mine!" Sam growled, his face inches from Cody's. His hands tightened on Cody's arms, nails digging in so hard they broke the skin. Cody struggled, trying to shove him off, but Sam was too strong. "You've always been mine!"

Cody let out a choked sound, panic filling his eyes as Sam's weight pressed down on him. "Get the fuck off me!"

Alen stumbled to his feet, heart pounding in his ears. "Sam, stop! Stop it!"

But Sam's eyes were dark, empty, like there was nothing left of the man they knew. His lips curled into a grin, teeth bared as he pinned Cody down.

"I've waited too long for this," Sam hissed, his breath hot against Cody's skin. His hands roamed over Cody's chest, too rough, too possessive, yanking at his shirt, ripping the fabric.

Cody's eyes went wide, terror flooding his face. "Get off me! Alen, help!"

Alen launched himself at Sam, grabbing him by the shoulders, trying to yank him off. But Sam didn't budge. His grip on Cody tightened, and he turned to Alen, eyes burning with rage.

"Stay the fuck out of this!" Sam snarled, throwing Alen back with a force that felt inhuman.

Alen hit the floor hard, gasping for breath as pain shot through his side. He struggled to get back up, but Sam—William—was already turning back to Cody, his fingers curling around Cody's throat.

"You're mine, James," Sam whispered, his voice low and trembling with excitement. "You've always been mine."

Chapter 20: All Hell Breaks Loose

The air was thick, choking, like it had weight to it. Cody's breath came in jagged bursts, the sound of his heart pounding so loud in his ears he could barely think straight. Sam, or whatever the fuck Sam had become, was still on the floor, that twisted grin plastered across his face, his eyes black as midnight.

Cody stumbled back, his chest tight, still gasping for air. The bruises on his throat throbbed, each breath a reminder that he'd barely escaped, for now.

Alen stood beside him, blood smeared across his nose and mouth. He still had the fire poker clutched in his hand, knuckles white. His breathing was just as shaky as Cody's, but his eyes were locked on Sam, waiting, watching for the next move. Sarah hovered near the doorway, frozen, her face pale as death, her hands trembling so hard they were practically shaking her whole body.

Sam groaned, rolling onto his knees, clutching his side where the poker had hit. But that grin... that fucking grin... it never left his face. "You think you're clever, don't you?" His voice was low, slick with malice, like oil dripping from his lips. "You think you can stop me?"

"Stay the fuck down, Sam," Alen snapped, his voice shaking. But there was no confidence behind it, only fear. "Just... stay down."

Sam's head lifted slowly, his dark, lifeless eyes locking onto Alen, and a low chuckle escaped him. "Why would I? This is just getting started." His voice twisted, deepened, like there were two voices coming out of his throat, Sam's and something else. "We've got all night."

"Sam, please," Sarah whispered, taking a shaky step forward, her hands raised like she could calm him, like they were dealing with a wild animal and not the demon wearing their friend's skin. "You're... you're scaring us. Just—just stop. You're not yourself."

Sam's grin widened, his teeth bared in a feral sneer. He stood slowly, towering over them now, his shoulders squared, eyes darting from one of them to the next. "I've never felt more like myself."

Alen's hand tightened around the fire poker, his pulse hammering in his throat. He wanted to move, to act, but he didn't know what the hell he could do. This wasn't just Sam anymore. This was something *else*. Something old, something evil.

"Get out of his head!" Cody spat, his voice hoarse, filled with desperation. "You want me, right? You keep calling me James? Fine, take me—just let him go!"

Sam's—or William's—eyes flickered toward Cody, his grin softening into something almost... tender. "You've always been mine, James. You were always supposed to be mine." His voice dropped, and it was dripping with that same twisted affection, the kind that crawled under your skin and rotted you from the inside. "But you let him get between us."

Cody's stomach twisted, bile rising in his throat. He took a step back, shaking his head. "I'm not James, Sam. You're confused—this house is fucking with your mind."

Sam took a step forward, his movements slow, deliberate, as if savoring the moment. "Oh, I know who you are. I've known for a long time." He paused, his fingers flexing. "You're the reason we're here. You, James. You betrayed me."

Cody felt his legs weaken beneath him, his body screaming to run, to fight, to do anything but stand there frozen. His eyes darted to Alen, silently begging for help, but Alen wasn't moving either—his face locked in an expression of shock and disbelief.

"Sam," Alen finally croaked, stepping forward. "This isn't you, man. You gotta snap out of this—this... thing's using you. Fight it."

Sam—or William—laughed, a sharp, jagged sound that echoed through the room. "Fight it? You think I want to fight it?" He raised his hand, and for the first time, Alen saw the blood, the red streaks smeared across Sam's fingers from when he'd dug his nails into Cody's skin. "I don't want to fight anymore."

And then, without warning, he lunged.

Sam's hands wrapped around Alen's throat before anyone could react, his face inches from Alen's, that grin stretching wider, more manic, more fucking wrong. "You think you can stop me?" he hissed, his fingers tightening, squeezing.

Alen gasped, his hands flying up, grabbing at Sam's wrists, trying to pry them off, but Sam's strength—William's strength—was inhuman. It was like trying to rip steel apart with bare hands. Alen's vision blurred, black spots dancing in front of his eyes as the air was crushed from his lungs.

"Alen!" Sarah screamed, rushing forward, her hands grabbing Sam's arm, pulling, clawing, trying to break his grip. "Let him go!"

Sam's head snapped toward her, his eyes wild, and he backhanded her across the face so hard that she crumpled to the floor, her head smacking the hardwood with a sickening thud.

Cody's heart leapt into his throat. "No!" He lunged, grabbing the poker from the floor, and swung with everything he had.

The metal collided with the side of Sam's head, the impact reverberating up Cody's arm. Sam staggered back, his grip loosening on Alen's throat, giving him just enough time to collapse to the floor, coughing and wheezing, struggling to breathe.

But Sam—William—didn't fall. He barely flinched. He turned toward Cody slowly, a low, dangerous growl building in his throat. His eyes, black as tar, narrowed on him. "That's not going to save you."

"Fuck you," Cody spat, brandishing the poker like a weapon, though his hands shook so badly he could barely keep it steady. "You're not him, Sam. You're not fucking Sam anymore."

Sam took a slow, deliberate step forward, his eyes never leaving Cody's. "You always did like to fight, James. You never knew when to stop."

Cody felt the bile rise in his throat again, but he didn't back down, even though every instinct was screaming at him to run. "You wanna kill me? Fine. But I'm not going down easy."

Sam's lips curled into that same sick, twisted smile. "Good." He lunged again, fast, too fast for Cody to react.

Sam's fist crashed into Cody's chest, knocking the wind out of him, sending him flying backward. He hit the floor hard, the back of his head slamming against the wood, his vision swimming. The poker clattered out of his hand, spinning across the room.

Sam was on him in an instant, hands grabbing his shirt, yanking him up, slamming him against the wall. "You were always mine," he snarled, his breath hot against Cody's face. His fingers dug into Cody's skin, hard enough to bruise, hard enough to break.

Cody's breath hitched, panic clawing at his throat, his hands scrambling to push Sam away, but it was no use. Sam's weight pinned him down, and his strength was overwhelming, demonic.

Alen, still gasping for air, struggled to his knees, his head pounding, his chest burning with every breath. He could see Cody struggling beneath Sam's grip, could hear him gasping for air, and for a moment, his mind went blank.

Then, with all the strength he had left, Alen lunged forward, grabbing the poker and swinging it with everything he had left. The metal connected with Sam's back, hard enough to send him stumbling forward, finally breaking his grip on Cody.

Cody collapsed to the floor, coughing violently, his throat burning, but he was alive.

Sam—or William—stood up slowly, his head tilting unnaturally, a slow smile curling across his lips as he turned toward Alen. "You just don't give up, do you?"

Alen's heart hammered in his chest, his hands trembling. He had nothing left. No strength. No fight. And Sam—William—was still standing, still grinning, still hungry.

"You're not gonna win this," Alen choked, raising the poker again, though his arms were shaking so hard he could barely hold it.

"Oh," William growled, his voice dripping with venom. "I already have."

Before Alen could react, Sam lunged at him again, his hands grabbing Alen by the throat, slamming him into the wall so hard the wood splintered around them. Alen's vision went white with pain, and then—darkness.

Chapter 21: Splintered

The house groaned and shuddered, the floor beneath their feet shifting like it had a mind of its own. Cody, Sarah, and Alen huddled together, hearts pounding, barely able to breathe after the chaos of Sam's violent outburst. The cold was seeping in from every wall, like the house itself was alive, watching them, feeding on their fear.

Cody helped Alen to his feet, his hand gripping the fire poker tightly, knuckles white. Sarah stayed close, her breath coming in shallow bursts, eyes wide, darting from shadow to shadow. The air was thick with tension, the weight of it pressing down on all of them.

Sam had disappeared into the shadows, leaving them in a house that felt more like a trap than shelter. The walls were breathing. The air smelled like rot, something old and foul, hidden deep within the bones of the place. Cody's mind raced. Where the fuck had Sam gone?

Then, they heard it—a soft groan, coming from down the hall.

"Sam," Sarah whispered, her voice trembling. "Is that him?"

Cody moved toward the sound, his heartbeat thudding painfully in his chest. "Stay behind me," he muttered, stepping forward. Each step felt like he was walking into a nightmare he couldn't wake up from.

And there, slumped against the wall, was Sam. His chest was rising and falling, his skin pale and drenched in sweat. But something was different. His eyes—when he opened them—were no longer that dark, terrifying black.

It was just... Sam.

Sam blinked slowly, like he was waking from a nightmare, his hands trembling as they pressed against the cold, hard floor. His breath was ragged, uneven, his body trembling with exhaustion. He looked up at them—lost. The darkness, the inhuman presence that had been controlling him, was gone.

"Sam?" Cody's voice was sharp, wary, the fire poker still gripped in his hand. He didn't move closer.

Sam's gaze flickered to Cody, his eyes wet with something close to fear, and he nodded weakly. "It's me... I think it's me."

Cody stepped forward cautiously, the muscles in his shoulders tight with tension. "What happened, man? Where did you go?"

Sam swallowed hard, his throat dry, like every word was costing him something. "He's gone. The... the thing inside me. The demon. It's not me. I swear to you, Cody, it was never me."

Sarah crouched beside Sam, her hands hovering over him, not sure if she should touch him. Her voice was soft, full of disbelief. "Sam, what the hell is going on? Who's doing this?"

Sam's breath hitched, his chest heaving like he was about to break. "It's not me. It's this fucking place. The house... it's the house."

Cody felt a cold wave wash over him, his grip on the poker loosening. "What do you mean, 'the house'? What's it doing to us?"

Sam's eyes glazed over for a second, and then he looked directly at Cody, his voice hoarse but clear. "While that... thing was inside me, I saw him. I saw everything. William. The house trapped him here. It's doing to me what it did to him."

The air around them seemed to still. The house, which had been creaking and groaning like it was alive, suddenly went deathly quiet. A cold wind swept through the room, and the temperature dropped even further. Cody's breath fogged in the freezing air, his heart hammering in his chest.

Then, from the darkness, a figure slowly materialized.

It wasn't Sam. It wasn't a demon. It was... William.

His translucent form flickered in the dim light, his face pale, his eyes dark and hollow. He looked young, though time had clearly done something to him, warped him. His expression was filled with regret—and sorrow.

Cody's grip on the poker tightened instinctively. "Who the fuck is that?"

"William," Sam whispered, his voice barely audible. "That's him. The real William."

William's voice, when he spoke, was soft and distant, like he was speaking from the past. "I never wanted this," he said, his words hanging in the cold air. "I never meant for it to happen like this."

Sarah backed up, her body trembling. "What... what do you mean? You're the one doing this, aren't you? You're the one that's been controlling Sam."

William shook his head slowly, the weight of his actions etched into his face. "No. It's not me. It's the house. The demon inside it. It... it took everything from me. Made me do things... terrible things."

Cody's stomach turned. He could feel the heaviness in the air, the truth of William's words sinking in. "What did it make you do?"

William's voice wavered as he spoke, his form flickering in and out of sight. "I came here with him. James. We were in love. This house was supposed to be our escape from the world. But the house—it... changed me. It twisted everything."

Cody felt a shiver crawl down his spine. *James. William thinks I'm James.*

William continued, his voice filled with pain. "It started small—just whispers at first. The house... it talks to you. It knows your fears, your desires. It uses them against you." He paused, his hands trembling. "It took me over. I tried to fight it, but I was weak. And it made me... kill him."

Sarah's breath hitched. "What... what happened?"

"I loved him," William whispered, his voice cracking. "But the house... the demon inside it. It made me see him as a threat. It made me think he was going to leave me. So I grabbed the gun... and I shot him."

Cody felt his stomach twist, bile rising in his throat. He could see it playing out in his mind—William, standing over James with a gun, possessed, helpless to stop himself. "And then you... killed yourself?"

William nodded, his face full of despair. "It wasn't me. The demon... it had already won. It used my hands, my body, just like it's doing with Sam. After I shot James, it turned the gun on me. We both died here. Trapped."

The room seemed to constrict, the air thickening, becoming harder to breathe. Cody could feel it—the house watching them, feeding on their fear.

Suddenly, the house groaned, and the floor beneath them trembled. The temperature dropped even more, and the shadows on the walls shifted unnaturally. The demon was still there—still in the house.

"We need to move," Cody said, his voice tight with urgency. "If this place is alive, then it's not gonna let us out easy."

But before they could act, the walls shuddered violently, and the floor between them split with a loud crack. Cody and Sarah were thrown to one side, while Sam—still shaking—and Alen were pushed toward the other.

"No!" Sarah screamed, her voice raw with panic. "Cody!"

"Stay where you are!" Cody yelled, trying to find another way around. "We'll meet back—just find a way out!"

The house was tearing them apart, physically separating them, the walls closing in like a predator cornering its prey.

In the other room, Sam was breathing hard, sweat dripping down his face as he leaned against the wall. Alen, still weak but conscious, watched him warily. The tension between them was thick, palpable.

"You alright?" Alen asked, his voice strained. He could see the fear in Sam's eyes, the way his hands shook as he fought to keep control.

Sam shook his head, his voice trembling. "I can feel it... it's still here. Inside me. The demon... it's not done yet."

Alen's heart pounded. "You can fight it, Sam. You have to."

But Sam's body stiffened suddenly, and his eyes rolled back in his head. His breath hitched as the demon began to claw its way back.

Alen felt his stomach drop. "Sam? Sam!"

For a moment, Sam's eyes flickered between black and their normal color, his hands clenching into fists as he fought against the possession.

And then, with a sudden burst of energy, Sam collapsed, his body going limp.

Chapter 22: Shattered

Cody's breath came in short bursts, his throat tight with tension as he moved cautiously through the dark hallway. The floorboards groaned under his feet, the old wood barely able to support his weight. Beside him, Sarah clutched his arm, her fingers cold and trembling. The air was thick, almost suffocating, with the smell of mold and something worse, something rotten, like death lingering just out of sight.

"Where the hell are we?" Cody muttered, his voice low, the fear creeping in. He glanced around at the decayed walls, the peeling wallpaper hanging in strips like skin sloughing off a corpse.

"I don't know," Sarah whispered, her voice barely above a breath. "This place... it's changing. I swear to you, it wasn't like this when we got here."

Cody couldn't argue. The house felt alive, shifting, breathing, and every corner they turned revealed something new. Something worse. He wiped the sweat from his forehead, his hands shaking. He didn't want to admit how fucking terrified he was, but it was getting harder to hide it. His stomach churned, and that familiar knot of panic tightened in his chest.

"We just need to find a way back," he said, though even as the words left his mouth, they felt empty. Hollow. He wasn't sure if there was a way back.

The hallway stretched on, the light from their phone screens barely cutting through the thick, oppressive darkness. The air smelled damp, heavy with the stench of rot and something else, something foul, like the decay of a body left too long in the sun.

Suddenly, Sarah stopped dead in her tracks. Her grip on Cody's arm tightened, nails digging into his skin.

"Cody..." she whispered, her voice shaking.

Cody turned, following her gaze, his stomach dropping.

At the end of the hall, something moved.

It wasn't human—at least, not anymore. The figure was tall, hunched, its limbs unnaturally long and twisted, its skin stretched tight over bones that jutted out at odd angles. The face, if you could call it that, was distorted, grotesque, like someone had taken a human skull and melted it, leaving the features sagging and warped. Its eyes were black, hollow pits, and its mouth was twisted into an unnatural grin.

"What the fuck is that?" Cody hissed, his heart slamming in his chest.

Sarah shook her head, her breath hitching in her throat. "I don't know, but we need to get the hell out of here."

The thing at the end of the hall twitched, its body jerking unnaturally, like it was struggling to move, its limbs stiff and awkward. And then, with a low, wet growl, it began to move toward them.

"Run," Cody said, grabbing Sarah's hand and pulling her back down the hallway. "Run!"

They sprinted down the dark corridor, the creature's footsteps heavy behind them, the sound of its bones cracking with every movement. Cody's lungs burned, his muscles screaming, but he didn't stop. He couldn't stop. His mind was screaming, don't look back, but he could feel it, right behind them, close enough that he could almost smell the rot on its breath.

They reached a door at the end of the hallway, Cody slamming his shoulder against it as it burst open. They stumbled into the room, the door crashing shut behind them. Cody pressed his back against it, panting, his heart threatening to explode out of his chest.

Sarah collapsed against the wall, her chest heaving. "What the fuck was that thing?" she gasped, her voice shaking.

Cody shook his head, wiping sweat from his brow. "I don't know. I don't wanna know. But we need to keep moving before it—"

Suddenly, a loud crash came from outside the door, followed by the sound of nails scratching against the wood. Cody froze, his blood running cold as the door shook violently.

"Shit, shit, shit," he muttered, looking around the room for something to block the door with.

The door shuddered again, this time harder, and a long, inhuman growl rumbled from the other side. Cody's pulse spiked, his vision narrowing, the panic tightening its grip around his throat.

"We need to block it," he said, his voice strained. "Help me."

They grabbed an old, rotting dresser from the corner of the room, shoving it against the door just as the wood splintered, the creature's claws bursting through.

"Go, go!" Cody yelled, pulling Sarah toward the other door at the far end of the room.

They crashed through it into another long, dark hallway, the air cold and damp. Cody could barely catch his breath, his chest tight, heart racing. The walls here were covered in old, faded portraits, the eyes of the figures following them as they ran.

"They're watching us," Sarah whispered, glancing at the portraits, her voice cracking with fear.

"Don't look," Cody muttered, grabbing her arm and pulling her along. "Just keep moving."

As they ran, something changed. The temperature dropped, and the smell of rot intensified. Cody's stomach lurched. The hallway stretched out longer than it should've—unnatural, like it was twisting, playing tricks on their minds.

Suddenly, they turned a corner and skidded to a stop.

Standing in front of them was a group of figures, grotesque and twisted, like the one they had seen before. Their bodies were mangled, some missing limbs, others with skin hanging loosely from their bones.

Their faces were barely recognizable as human, distorted and twisted into expressions of pain and suffering.

One of them took a step forward, its mouth hanging open in a silent scream. Another figure moved behind it, dragging itself along the floor, its legs twisted and broken.

"Cody..." Sarah whimpered, backing up against the wall.

"I see them," Cody whispered, his voice barely there. "Just... don't make a sound."

But the figures moved closer, their eyes black and empty, their bodies jerking unnaturally, like puppets on strings. They seemed to be searching for something, their movements slow and deliberate.

One of the figures turned toward them, its head cocked at an odd angle, its mouth slowly curling into that same grotesque grin they had seen before.

Suddenly, the walls began to shudder, and Cody felt the floor beneath his feet shift. He grabbed Sarah's arm, trying to pull her with him, but before he could react, the hallway split, a loud crack echoing through the house as the floor gave way between them.

"Cody!" Sarah screamed, her voice full of panic as she stumbled back, trying to reach him.

"Sarah!" Cody yelled, lunging forward, but it was too late. The floor had separated them, the gap widening until it became a gaping chasm of darkness.

"Stay there!" Cody shouted, his heart pounding in his throat. "I'll find a way to you—just don't move!"

Sarah's face was pale, her body trembling as she backed away from the grotesque figures that were now turning toward her, their empty eyes locking onto her. She looked back at Cody, her voice shaking with terror.

"Cody... I don't think I'm alone."

Cody's blood ran cold. He could see the figures closing in on her, their movements slow but deliberate, their mouths opening and closing in silent screams. The air around her seemed to ripple, like something unseen was lurking just beneath the surface, waiting to strike.

"Stay calm, Sarah," Cody whispered, trying to keep his voice steady. "I'll get to you. Just... stay calm."

But Sarah's eyes were wide with terror, her breath coming in short, panicked bursts. "Cody... they're coming."

"Fuck!" Cody slammed his fist against the wall, his body shaking with helplessness as he watched the figures close in on her.

The house was alive. It was playing with them, separating them, making them easy prey. And there was nothing Cody could do but watch as Sarah's scream echoed down the hallway, swallowed by the darkness.

Chapter 23: Shadows in the Past

Sam leaned against the wall, his breath still ragged but steadier now. His skin was pale, sweat slicking his brow, but he was coming back to himself. The house wasn't crawling under his skin, not like before. Alen, next to him, looked just as bad, blood still trickling from the side of his head, though he was too stubborn to admit it hurt.

"How you holding up, man?" Alen asked, his voice low but shaky, like he was trying to hold it together.

Sam wiped his face with the back of his hand, sucking in air. "I'm fine, at least for now." His eyes flickered with uncertainty, but he wasn't about to fall apart again. "We gotta keep moving."

Alen nodded, though he winced as he straightened up. "Yeah, and find Cody and Sarah. This place is trying to split us up for good." He glanced around, the dim light flickering through cracks in the walls, casting long shadows that seemed to crawl.

The hallway stretched on, impossibly long, doorways lining the walls as they walked by. Each room looked like it had been frozen in time—furniture rotting, dust settled thick over everything. Something was off, though. Too quiet. Too still.

They came to a door, heavier than the others. Sam hesitated, his hand hovering over the knob. He didn't want to open it. Something on the other side was waiting.

"Open it," Alen said, his voice soft but firm.

Sam twisted the knob, pushing the door open slowly. The room beyond was dark, but not completely. A faint light filtered through a stained glass window, casting eerie shadows across the floor. The air inside smelled of mold, old wood, and something sour, like the stench of old blood.

Alen took a step forward, eyes scanning the space. "What is this place?"

Before Sam could answer, something shifted. Alen froze mid-step. His breath caught, his heart pounding in his ears. The room around him seemed to dim, the walls twisting, the light growing faint.

Suddenly, he wasn't there anymore.

He was standing in a different room. The light was dim, flickering from a single candle set on a table near the window. The air was thick, suffocating. There was a man in front of him—Robert Morrow, Alen's mind whispered, though he had no idea where the name came from. He knew it just as well as if the man had spoken it aloud. Robert looked to be in his late 30s, his dark hair slicked back, his shirt stained with sweat. His face was gaunt, eyes wild, his jaw clenched tight like he was holding back a scream.

Robert had once been a schoolteacher, though that life felt distant now. He'd come to the house seeking refuge from a life he didn't want, escaping debts and mistakes. His wife had left him after he'd lost everything in a series of bad investments, and the drinking hadn't helped. The house was supposed to be a place to start over—a quiet place to get his head straight—but it had quickly turned into his prison. He'd been trapped for months, unable to leave, the walls whispering to him, his sanity slipping with each passing day. Now, he was nothing but a frightened shell of the man he used to be.

Alen's body felt frozen, rooted in place as Robert stumbled backward, glancing toward the door. He was trapped, just like Alen was. The hopelessness on his face was suffocating, the dread making it hard to breathe.

The room trembled. The walls shifted, like the house was breathing, closing in. Robert gasped, his hands going to his throat, trying to scream, but no sound came out.

And then it happened.

Robert's body jerked, his arms twisting violently to the side. Alen's heart raced as he watched, helpless, unable to look away. Robert let out a choked cry, his body contorting unnaturally as his skin began to stretch. It started at his chest, splitting open with a wet, sickening tear. Alen's stomach lurched, his pulse racing.

Robert's scream finally broke free, piercing the silence, filling the room with a high, desperate wail. His arms twisted behind him, bones snapping like dry twigs as his legs began to bend, folding backward until the bones broke through the skin.

Blood sprayed across the floor, hot and thick, pooling beneath him. Robert was trembling, his mouth wide open, eyes wild with panic. His chest, ripped wide down the middle, pulsed, his ribs splitting open like a grotesque flower, bone and muscle pulling apart in slow, deliberate agony.

The house was tearing him in half.

His body shook violently, his back arching as the house forced him down, splitting him even further. His organs spilled from the open cavity, splattering onto the floor with a dull, wet thud. Robert tried to scream again, but his throat was already tearing apart, the sound choking off as blood poured from his mouth, thick and dark.

Alen could feel it all—the raw pain, the suffocating weight of terror crushing Robert's lungs. His vision blurred as Robert's legs twisted violently, the bones snapping again, louder this time. Flesh peeled away from his body like wet paper, bones splintering as the house twisted him apart piece by piece.

Suddenly, with a final, brutal crack, Robert's body ripped completely in half. Blood sprayed across the walls, painting the room in a thick, visceral red. His eyes rolled back in his head, his mouth hanging open in silent horror as his two halves fell to the ground with a sickening thud, his insides spilling out like a broken doll.

The room was drenched in blood. It dripped from the ceiling, pooled in the cracks of the floor. Robert's body lay in pieces, his face frozen in the last moments of agonized terror.

Alen stood there, breathing hard, feeling his own heart pounding in his chest. The vision held him there, locked in place, unable to tear himself away from the horror that had just unfolded. His breath came in short, panicked gasps, his mind racing. He could still hear the echoes of Robert's screams, could feel the wet, sticky warmth of the blood coating the floor beneath him.

Then, just as suddenly as it had started, the room snapped back into the present. The blood was gone, Robert was gone. He was back in the dark, dusty study with Sam, who was shaking him, his voice sharp with panic.

"Alen, snap out of it. What the hell's going on?"

Alen blinked, his breath catching in his throat. His heart was still racing, his body trembling. He looked down at his hands, expecting to see them covered in blood, but they were clean. Dry.

"What the fuck just happened?" Sam asked, his voice low but urgent.

Alen couldn't speak. His mouth was dry, his body still shaking from the vision. He wiped a trembling hand across his face, trying to make sense of it.

"I... I saw someone," Alen muttered, his voice hoarse. "His name was Robert Morrow. The house... it split him in half. He was screaming, and there was so much blood. It... it was real, Sam. I was there."

Sam's face tightened, his eyes dark with worry. "Jesus. We need to get out of here."

Alen nodded, though his legs felt like jelly. His breath was still coming in shallow bursts, his heart racing with the memory of what he had just seen. "Yeah... let's move."

They turned toward the door, but as they did, the air around them seemed to grow heavier, thicker. The temperature plummeted, and from the darkness beyond the door, they heard it—a low, wet sound, like something moving in the shadows.

Sam's pulse spiked, his breath catching in his throat. They weren't alone.

Chapter 24: Alone

Sarah hugged herself tight, her arms trembling as she moved down the hallway. The old wood creaked under her feet, every step slow, dragging. The air felt heavy, pressing in on her chest, sticking in her lungs. Her skin was damp with cold sweat, and no matter how hard she tried to calm herself, her hands wouldn't stop shaking.

"Come on, Sarah," she muttered, her voice barely audible over her own footsteps. "Get a grip. Just keep moving. You're fine. You'll find them."

But she didn't feel fine. Not even close. The house was too quiet, like it was waiting for her to crack. Every creak made her heart jump, every shadow looked like it was shifting. She was alone. Completely alone.

"Where are they?" she whispered again, to no one. Her pulse pounded in her ears, her breathing uneven. "Cody... Sam... anyone?"

Nothing. Silence. The air hung thick with dust and something sour, like mold or rot. Her stomach twisted. She felt like the walls were closing in, like the house was watching her, waiting for her to lose it.

She stopped, leaning against the wall, closing her eyes for a second. "This is crazy," she muttered. "I'm talking to myself. Losing it. Just keep going."

Then she heard it. Something faint. A soft whisper. Her eyes snapped open, her breath catching in her throat. She stood still, listening. The whisper came again, low, too quiet to make out but enough to send a chill through her body. And then, she heard something else, a wet dragging sound.

"Who's there?" Her voice cracked as she spun around, her eyes wide, scanning the dark.

Nothing. The hallway behind her was empty, stretched out and still. But that sound, the dragging, it was getting closer. Louder. Something was moving.

She took a step back, her heart hammering in her chest. "This isn't real," she whispered, her voice barely audible. "It's just the house messing with me."

But the dragging didn't stop. It grew heavier, closer. Something wet and heavy scraping along the floor. Her pulse raced, skin prickling with fear. She turned again, eyes darting through the shadows.

Then she saw it.

Something moved down the hall. A man, or at least it had been. Half a man. His body was split from the waist down, dragging itself across the floor. His arms pulled him forward, his hands leaving bloody smears. His face was twisted, gaunt, his eyes wide, frozen in a mix of fear and pain. Blood leaked from his mouth, thick and dark. His whole body jerked with each pull.

Sarah's breath hitched, her legs locking up. "No... this can't be real."

The man dragged himself closer, one hand reaching out, fingers bent and broken, dripping with blood. His eyes locked onto hers, wide, unblinking, staring through her. His mouth twitched, as if trying to speak.

"Help me..." the whisper came, wet and thick, but his mouth didn't move. "Help me..."

She stumbled back, bile rising in her throat. "No, stay the fuck away from me," she gasped, but her voice was weak, barely above a whisper. Her heart pounded so hard it hurt.

The man dragged himself forward again, his bloodied body making a sickening sound as it scraped the floor. His intestines trailed behind him, glistening, the smell of rot filling the air.

"Help me..." the whisper came again. His eyes, wide, pleading.

She couldn't move. She couldn't breathe. He wasn't real, her mind screamed, but the closer he got, the harder it was to believe.

"Help me..." his voice cracked, his face twisting in agony. But his lips never moved. The whisper just filled the hallway, pressing down on her, making her legs shake.

Her back hit the wall, and she gasped, panic taking over. "Please... no... just stay away."

The man's body jerked again, bones cracking as he pulled himself closer. His hand reached for her, blood dripping from his fingers, inches from her now. She could smell it, the thick stench of decay and blood.

Then he stopped. His body trembled, his face contorting into a grotesque grin. His eyes stayed locked on hers, his voice barely a whisper now, softer, more desperate.

"Help me..." he said again, and then he collapsed. His body went still. The dragging stopped, and the hallway went quiet.

Sarah stood frozen, her chest heaving, breath coming in ragged gasps. Her back pressed hard against the wall. This wasn't real. It couldn't be.

She squeezed her eyes shut, tears burning the corners. "Go away... just go away..."

When she opened her eyes again, he was gone. The hallway was empty, silent, but the smell of blood and rot still lingered in the air.

Her hands were shaking as she pushed herself off the wall, her legs unsteady beneath her. "I... I need to find Cody," she whispered. "I need to get out of here."

Chapter 25: The Wrong Sam

Cody moved through the dim hallway, his heart pounding as he called out, "Sarah? Sarah, where the hell are you?" His voice echoed back, swallowed up by the dead air. Sweat trickled down his forehead, and he wiped it away, trying to keep calm. The walls felt too close, and the air was heavy, making it harder to breathe. This house was alive, and it was toying with them. Tearing them apart.

He replayed it in his mind. One second, Sarah had been right next to him, and the next—everything went to hell.

The house had shuddered, the walls vibrating like something was waking up inside them. Cody remembered the way the floor shifted under his feet, and how, in a flash, a crack split the hallway in two. He'd grabbed for Sarah, but the floor opened up between them.

"Cody!" Sarah had screamed, stumbling back as the gap between them widened into a dark chasm.

"Sarah!" Cody had lunged, but it was too late. The floor had separated them. He'd been left standing there, breathless, staring at the void that swallowed her.

Now, he was alone. But he was going to find her, no matter what.

As he rounded another corner, he saw a figure step out of the shadows.

"Cody?"

Cody jumped, heart pounding as he turned toward the voice. "Sam?" he breathed in relief. "Man, I thought I was the only one left. Where the hell have you been?"

Sam stepped closer, his expression unreadable. "Looking for you, man. This house... I don't know, it's doing something, but I found you, didn't I?"

Cody let out a shaky breath, his shoulders dropping. "Yeah, this place... it's messed up. One minute, Sarah's right there, and then the next, the fuckin' floor splits open. I couldn't reach her. One second she was there, the next she was gone. You seen Alen?"

Sam shook his head. "No. I lost him too. But we'll find them."

Cody nodded, though his nerves were still buzzing. He fell into step next to Sam, grateful for the company, but his heart still raced from the thought of Sarah out there, lost somewhere in this twisted house.

The hallway stretched on in silence, the dim light casting long shadows that seemed to shift and move. The air felt heavier with each step they took. The walls, the floor, everything about this place felt wrong.

"So, what's the plan?" Cody asked, breaking the silence. "You got any idea where the hell they might be?"

Sam shrugged. "No clue. This place is a maze. But we'll figure it out. We've got time."

Cody glanced at him, a weird sense of unease creeping in. "Time? What the hell does that mean? We need to get outta here. Find Sarah, find Alen, and get the hell out."

Sam smiled, but there was something about it that made Cody's skin crawl. "What's the rush?"

Cody blinked, stopping in his tracks. "What do you mean, what's the rush? You wanna stay here or something?"

Sam stopped too, turning to face Cody. "I'm just saying... wouldn't it be nice if we didn't have to rush? Just take it easy. You and me. Here."

Cody's stomach twisted. "What? No, man, we need to—"

Sam stepped closer, his voice dropping lower. "I mean, come on. You and me, Cody. Just us. Doesn't that sound... nice?"

Cody stared at him, his pulse quickening. Something wasn't right. "Sam, what the hell are you talking about?"

Sam smiled again, that weird smile stretching wider. "Why are you so tense? Relax. We're fine. You don't have to be scared. Not with me."

Cody's gut churned, every instinct screaming at him that something was wrong, but he couldn't figure it out. "Sam... what's going on with you, man?"

Sam's eyes glinted in the dim light, his smile soft but unsettling. "Nothing's wrong, Cody. I'm just... feeling good. You know? Kinda frisky." His voice was smooth, casual. "Wanna have some fun?"

Cody's blood ran cold. This wasn't Sam.

He backed up, his hands shaking. "What the fuck is wrong with you? Get away from me."

Sam stepped forward, the strange smile never leaving his face. "Why are you backing away? You don't have to run. It's just us, Cody. We're good."

Cody turned and bolted.

His feet pounded against the floor as he ran down the hall, his breath coming in ragged bursts. He didn't know where he was going—he just had to get away. His heart was slamming in his chest, his mind spinning with panic.

But Sam was fast. Too fast.

Cody barely made it around the corner before he grabbed him, yanking him backward. He hit the floor hard, the wind knocked out of him. Before he could even react, Sam was on top of him, pinning him down with a force that wasn't human.

"Where you goin', Cody?" Sam's voice was soft, almost amused. He leaned down, his face inches from Cody's, his breath hot and foul. Cody's stomach churned as the stench hit him—a rotting, sick smell, like something long dead. Sam's face hovered over him, but it was changing now. His skin, sagging, pulling away, his eyes darkening, hollowing out.

Cody struggled, panic gripping him. "Get the fuck off me!"

Sam—or whatever it was—grinned, his mouth pulling into something grotesque, his teeth yellowed and sharp. "Why you fighting it, Cody?" he whispered, his voice rasping, almost playful. "It's just us. No need to be scared."

Cody's heart pounded, his mind racing. This wasn't Sam. His breath hitched as he felt the weight of the thing crushing him, suffocating him.

"You're mine, Cody," the thing whispered, its voice deep and cold. The smell of rot filled Cody's nose, making him gag. "Always been mine."

Cody shut his eyes tight, his chest heaving, panic racing through him. He could feel the thing's breath on his face, the rot, the decay, making his stomach turn.

Then, silence.

The weight lifted. The smell faded.

Cody opened his eyes slowly, his body shaking. Sam was gone. The hallway was empty, like nothing had happened. His breath came in short, gasping bursts, his heart still pounding in his chest.

He lay there, staring up at the ceiling, his mind reeling. In the distance, from somewhere deep in the house, a voice echoed, low and cold.

"Soon, Cody... soon."

Chapter 26: Something New

Alen and Sam turned toward the door, but the air around them grew heavy, like the walls themselves were closing in. The temperature dropped sharply, and from the darkness beyond the door, they heard it, a low, wet sound, like something slithering through the shadows.

Sam's breath hitched in his throat. "Alen, we're not alone," he whispered, his voice shaky.

The sound crept closer, the unmistakable noise of something dragging itself along the floor. Alen's stomach turned, his body freezing in place. He could feel it, whatever was beyond that door, it was alive, waiting.

"We need to go," Sam muttered, his eyes wide, his feet shuffling backward. "We need to get the fuck out of here."

Alen nodded, but his legs wouldn't move. His heart hammered in his chest, the cold air biting at his skin. The door creaked open, the hinges groaning, and something emerged from the darkness.

It was crawling, twisted, broken, and dragging itself across the floor with sickening effort. Its limbs were bent at angles that no human body could survive, the bones poking through thin, gray skin. A slick, wet sound accompanied each movement, like it was covered in something thick and sticky.

Sam stumbled back, pressing against the wall, his breath coming in short, panicked bursts. "What the fuck is that?"

Alen's throat tightened. He couldn't tear his eyes away from it. The thing's face, or what was left of it, was a mangled mess of skin and bone, half of it missing, revealing glistening, blackened muscle. One of its eyes hung loose, dangling from a thread, its mouth open in a twisted, unnatural grin.

"Help... me..." The voice that came from it was broken, gurgling, like it was trying to speak through a throat full of liquid. "Please... help..."

Alen gagged, bile rising in his throat. He wanted to run, but his feet were rooted to the floor. His mind screamed at him to move, to get away from this thing, but he couldn't.

The creature dragged itself closer, the wet, slick sound of its body scraping the floor filling the air. Its eyes, or eye locked onto Alen, its hand outstretched, fingers clawing at the ground.

"Alen, move!" Sam yelled, his voice trembling. "We need to go!"

Before either of them could move, the room shifted. The walls seemed to breathe, closing in, the floor groaning beneath their feet. And then, the world around them changed.

They were no longer in the hallway.

The room was small and dark, the air cold, so cold it hurt to breathe. The walls were damp, the floor creaking under their weight. An old, rotting bed sat in the corner, its mattress torn, stained with dark, dried blood. The stench of decay was overwhelming, thick and suffocating.

But it was the figure in the middle of the room that made Alen's heart stop.

A woman, her body suspended from the ceiling by her wrists. Her arms were twisted behind her, her legs hanging limp, her head bent forward. Her clothes were torn, her skin pale, blue, as if all the life had been drained from her.

Sam gasped, his voice barely above a whisper. "What the fuck is this?"

Alen's stomach turned, his eyes wide. "This can't be real."

The woman's body jerked violently, her head snapping up, her eyes wide and wild with terror. Blood dripped from her mouth, and she let out a choked scream, the sound echoing through the small room.

Before Alen could react, her arms started to stretch, pulling her shoulders from their sockets with a sickening crack. The skin on her arms tore, blood running down her sides as her bones bent and snapped under the weight.

Her legs kicked wildly, her body thrashing as she tried to scream again, but no sound came out. Just a horrible, wet gurgling noise, blood pouring from her mouth as she convulsed in the air.

"Alen... we need to go," Sam whispered, his voice trembling with fear. "We need to get the fuck out of here, now."

Alen tried to move, but he was frozen, his eyes locked on the woman's contorted, broken body. Her legs bent in impossible directions, bones cracking, flesh tearing. Blood poured onto the floor, thick and black, pooling beneath her.

Her chest heaved, and with a violent jerk, her ribs snapped, cracking open like dry wood. Her torso split, her organs spilling out onto the floor in a steaming, bloody heap.

Alen stumbled back, his hand flying to his mouth as he gagged. The room stank of death, of blood and rot. The woman's body hung limp, her blood splattering across the room in slow, steady drips, like a heartbeat.

Sam grabbed Alen's arm, his grip tight. "We need to go. We need to fucking move!"

But Alen couldn't stop shaking, his mind reeling, his legs trembling beneath him. He was trapped, watching the horror unfold in front of him, helpless.

The woman's head fell forward again, her body still, the silence deafening. But the air was still thick, still cold. The room seemed to press in around them, suffocating them, like the house itself was alive.

Then, from the darkness, a voice whispered. It was low, barely audible, but it cut through the air like a knife.

"You can't leave. You're already mine."

Alen's breath caught in his throat. He didn't dare look back. He didn't want to see what was waiting for them in the shadows.

Without another word, they ran.

Chapter 27: Cody's Fear

Cody's breathing was uneven, every inhale sharp like he couldn't get enough air. His flashlight flickered again, casting jagged, shifting shadows along the walls that seemed to reach for him. This house was fucking with him. Every sound felt alive, like it was watching, waiting to close in on him.

And Sarah was gone.

The floor had split, torn itself apart like the house had decided to pull them under. One second, she had been there, right beside him. The next? Swallowed by the dark.

"Sarah!" Cody yelled again, his voice cracking, bouncing off the walls. Nothing. Just silence. Just the endless, creeping dark.

His hand shook as he wiped the sweat from his forehead. His stomach felt twisted, knotted up. Too fucking quiet. And that was when the memory of Sam crawled back in, crawling under his skin like it had been waiting there.

Sam... or whatever the hell had been pretending to be Sam.

Cody forced himself to move forward, but he couldn't stop his mind from flashing back to that grin. That twisted, lazy smile on Sam's face. Like he was hiding something. Like he wasn't Sam anymore.

That wasn't Sam.

Couldn't be.

Sam had gotten too close, his breath hot and sour like something dead, whispering, "We don't have to leave, Cody... we could stay here. Just us. Forever."

Cody shuddered, his stomach churning, his skin crawling. That thing had worn Sam's face, but it wasn't him. No way. Not with the way Sam had looked at him. Hungry. Like he wanted something Cody didn't want to give.

"I've waited a long time for this, Cody."

Cody swallowed hard, rubbing his hands over his face. Fuck. What if he ran into Sam again? What if he couldn't get away this time? The thought made his legs feel weak, like they might give out any second.

But he had to find Sarah. Had to keep moving. He stepped into another room, the air colder here, staler. The smell of wet wood and rot hit him as soon as he crossed the threshold. His flashlight flickered over a dusty desk. Papers, books, and other clutter were scattered everywhere, but right in the middle of the mess was a journal.

It looked old. Very old.

Cody reached out with shaking hands and opened it. The name Robert Morrow was scribbled inside the front cover. April 1990. His throat tightened as he started reading.

The Diary of Robert Morrow

March 15, 1990

We finally moved in. Alastar Manor. It's huge, way bigger than I thought, and old as hell, but it's got potential. Helen's excited, running around, talking about curtains and where to put the furniture. She's happy, and honestly, that's what matters most.

Thomas... he's been quiet. He's 16, so I guess that's normal, right? But he's not as excited as us. Just spends most of his time by the window, staring out into the yard. I've asked him a few times if he's alright, and he just shrugs me off.

Helen says he's just adjusting to the new place. I hope she's right.

April 1, 1990

Thomas ran into the Livingroom today yelling that he saw a man go into his bedroom, he said he thought it was me but when he got to his door there was no one in the room. At first, I thought he was just playing an April Fools joke but when I saw the look in his eyes, I knew he wasn't. I went up but I saw no one in the room. I think maybe his imagination is getting the best of him

April 8, 1990

The house creaks a lot at night. I expected that—it's old. But last night, I heard something more than creaks. Footsteps. Slow, heavy footsteps. Helen woke up too. She swears someone was walking outside the bedroom. I got up to check, but the hall was empty. Just us.

Thomas is still quiet. I've caught him looking over his shoulder a few times, like he's nervous. I don't want to push him too much, but ever since he told us what he saw he's acted strange, like he is afraid of what might come nect. And to tell you the truth, so do I.

April 12, 1990

We went into town today, met some locals, grabbed some supplies. The people were friendly enough until I mentioned the house. Alastar Manor. That's when things got weird. The guy at the store, his smile disappeared. He just gave me this look and said, "I wouldn't stay there long if I were you. Strange things happen in that house."

Helen's been more spooked since. And the house? It's louder at night. The creaks sound different. It's like someone's moving around, but every time I check, there's no one there. Thomas... he's been quieter than ever. Won't talk about what's bothering him.

April 20, 1990

The house is changing. I don't know how to explain it, but the air feels heavier now. Like there's something in it. The windows won't open anymore. I tried to crack one for some air, but it's stuck. The phones aren't working either.

I asked Thomas what he thought, and he just said, "It feels wrong, Dad. The whole place, I don't like it and we need to move"

I wanted to reassure him, tell him everything would be fine. But the truth? I'm not sure anymore. But I sank every dime I have into this home, we can't move.

April 27, 1990

Helen woke up screaming last night. She swore there was someone in the room, standing at the foot of the bed. But when I turned on the light, it was just us.

The house is louder now. Not just at night, but all the time. The walls creak like they're... breathing. I don't know how else to describe it.

Thomas and I tried to break one of the windows today. I grabbed a hammer and smashed it with everything I had, but the glass didn't even crack. It's like it's not glass at all. The house won't let us out.

May 2, 1990

We found Helen today.

Thomas and I woke up, and she wasn't in bed. We looked everywhere, and then we found her in one of the unused bedrooms, hanging by her arms from the bedpost. Blood everywhere. Her body was twisted, bruised... like she'd been struggling.

Thomas screamed, it was all I could do to keep it together for my son, I finally calmed him down, "Thomas, we need to get her down" We cut her down and put her on the floor, she was dead, she had been tortured by someone, no...by something.

We took her body to the basement because where else could we put her? We're trapped in here. No one's coming to help. I tried the phone again, it's dead. We're stuck. I don't know what to do. My wife is dead now, I have to protect Thomas.

May 5, 1990

Thomas and I tried again today. We smashed the windows, kicked at the doors. Nothing worked. It's like the house is keeping us in.

He's scared, just as scared as I am. He said he keeps hearing voices, whispers from the walls. He said that sometimes he hears his mother calling to him. I hear them too.... I hear her... I didn't want to tell him that, but it's true. She is calling out, or something is.

We stay together all the time now, sometimes we here footsteps upstairs, but when I check the attic, it's empty. Every time.

May 10, 1990

We're falling apart. I'm falling apart. Thomas is trying to hold it together, but I see the fear in his eyes. He asked me today if we'd ever leave, if we'd ever make it out. I didn't have an answer for him.

I don't know how much longer we can last.

May 13, 1990

We got separated today.

One minute, Thomas was right behind me. The next? Gone. I screamed his name, ran through the halls, checked every room. But the house... it's like it swallowed him up. The house is alive. I know it. It's playing with us.

I can't lose him too. I won't.

May 15, 1990

My dad's dead.

I found him in the library this morning, torn in half. There was blood everywhere. On the walls, the floor. I don't even know how something like that can happen to a person.

I'm alone now. But I think I found a way out. There's a door in the basement, one I've never seen before. I don't know where it leads, but it's my only chance.

If someone finds this, don't stay. Don't try to fight it. Just Run.

Cody slammed the journal shut, his heart hammering in his chest, hands trembling. Thomas had gotten out. He must've.

But the house? It's alive. Cody could feel it, crawling under his skin, whispering through the walls. This house didn't let go. It twisted you up, chewed you through until there was nothing left.

His stomach churned, fear crawling up his throat, making his skin cold. His hands were shaking as he stood there, trying to breathe, trying to wrap his mind around what he'd just read. They had tried to get out. The Morrow family had done everything, and the house had taken them anyway. Cody hoped that Thomas had exapted the houses grasp, he hoped that he could find the door that Thomas was talking about. He had to.

Then he heard it again.

A voice. Soft. From the corner of the room.

"Cody..."

His blood went cold. Slowly, he turned, his flashlight shaking in his hand. The beam flickered through the dark, cutting through the shadows.

Nothing. Just darkness.

The voice came again, closer now. A whisper.

"Cody... I'm waiting for you."

Chapter 28: Cody's Descent

"I need to find the others," Cody muttered, slamming the diary shut. His hands were trembling, his pulse thudding hard in his ears. "I gotta tell them about this damn diary."

His chest felt tight, like there wasn't enough air. The family had been trapped, just like him. They had tried everything, but the house—it had swallowed them whole. Now they were gone, except maybe for Thomas, the one who had escaped. Cody held onto that thought like a lifeline. He needed to believe there was a way out, that someone had beaten this thing before. But first, he had to find the others. Sarah, Alen—they needed to know what he'd found.

He stepped out into the hallway, the cold air clinging to him, like a second skin. It felt darker now, the shadows thicker, longer. The flashlight beam flickered, the light bouncing off the warped walls. The creaks and groans of the house echoed through the silence, like it was alive, breathing all around him.

"Sarah? Alen?" Cody called out, his voice thin and shaky. No answer. The hallway stretched out in front of him, twisting, too long, like it was pulling him in.

"I just need to find them," he muttered again, almost like saying it would make them appear. "Gotta tell them what I found, figure out how we're gonna get the hell out of here."

His legs felt like jelly, but he forced himself to keep moving. Every step felt heavier. His mind kept drifting back to Sam, or whatever had been pretending to be Sam. That smile. Too slow, too easy, like Sam had known something Cody didn't. Worse, it felt like Sam had enjoyed watching him squirm.

What if he ran into him again? No, when he ran into him again. Because that thing wasn't done with him yet. Cody could feel it. His gut twisted at the thought. Could he even run fast enough this time? Fight? He wasn't sure.

The flashlight flickered as he stepped into another room. The air hit him like ice, colder than before, and it smelled wrong. The stench of rotting wood and something sour clung to him, making his stomach churn. His breath hitched as he scanned the room, the light bouncing off debris, a shattered mirror, and then... he saw her.

Sarah.

At first, he froze, blinking like his mind couldn't process what he was seeing. Sarah was just standing there, or what he thought was Sarah. But her body... it wasn't right. It was twisted, mangled like she had been through something violent. Her arms hung at weird angles, her legs buckled beneath her. And her face... Cody's heart skipped a beat.

Her face was... gone.

The skin had been ripped off, torn away, leaving nothing but raw, shredded flesh and bone. Cody's stomach turned. His knees almost gave out as he stumbled backward, his heart hammering in his chest. His breath caught in his throat, and he felt the bile rising up. But he couldn't take his eyes off her.

It looked like Sarah. Her clothes, her hair, it was all there. But no... it couldn't be her. It wasn't her. The house was playing tricks again, just like it had with Sam. This wasn't Sarah. It couldn't be.

He swallowed hard, his mouth dry, words barely leaving his lips. "No... no, no, no..." He shook his head, taking another shaky step back, his fingers tightening around the flashlight.

Sarah didn't move. She didn't make a sound. Her body just stood there, frozen like a doll, her mouth hanging open as if she had been screaming, but no noise came out. Cody's mind was racing, screaming at him to move, to do something, but he was stuck in place, staring at the horror in front of him.

Then her body twitched.

Cody's whole body jerked. His heart jumped into his throat. No. That wasn't real. It couldn't be. His eyes widened as he watched her arm twitch again, a sickening sound of bone scraping against the floor. Slowly, impossibly, Sarah's body began to move. First one arm, then the other, dragging herself forward, inch by inch. Her head lolled to the side, blood dripping from the torn skin where her face should have been.

Cody stumbled backward, almost tripping over himself. His breath came in short, panicked gasps, his pulse racing. He couldn't think, couldn't move. It was Sarah. It had to be. But no... the house. The house was doing this. It had to be the house pretending to be her.

He was on the ground now, the flashlight slipping from his grasp, the beam flickering weakly as it rolled away. The shadows grew longer, thicker, swallowing the room in darkness. Cody scrambled to his feet, but Sarah... or whatever it was... was getting closer.

"Sarah!" he shouted, but his voice cracked halfway through her name. His hands were shaking so hard he couldn't even grab the flashlight. His mind raced. *This isn't real. It's not her. It's not her...*

Then she spoke.

"Cody... help me."

Cody froze. His blood ran cold. That voice... it was Sarah's voice. He knew it, down to the way she said his name. But no, it couldn't be her. The house was screwing with him. It had to be. It had used Sam, and now it was doing the same with Sarah. This wasn't real. It couldn't be.

He tried to stand, but his legs felt like lead. "You're not real," Cody whispered, his voice trembling. "You're just this place, messing with me."

But she kept moving. Her mangled arms reached out toward him, fingers twitching as they dragged her broken body across the floor. It wasn't her, but it looked so much like her. Her clothes, her hair, everything except that... face. That absence of a face.

"Help me, Cody..." she whispered again, her voice softer now. Desperate. Broken.

Cody's chest tightened. His heart was racing so hard he thought it might tear itself apart. His eyes flicked to the door. He could still make it out, could still run. But he couldn't tear himself away from her. What if, somehow, some part of her was still in there? What if it really was Sarah?

"No..." Cody choked out, his hands shaking. He took a step back, almost stumbling over his own feet. "You're not... you can't be her."

Her body jerked violently, her head snapping up like she was being controlled by invisible strings. Her faceless form seemed to lock onto him, even though she had no eyes. Her movements were unnatural, sharp, her body twisting as she dragged herself closer, leaving a thick trail of blood behind her.

"Help me, Cody." Her voice was weak now, fragile. It sent a chill down his spine, but at the same time, it tugged at something inside him.

His mind was screaming at him to run. *This isn't real*, he kept telling himself, over and over, trying to push the thoughts away. But her voice... her voice kept him frozen. *What if it really was her?*

"I'm sorry," Cody whispered, his voice breaking. "I can't..."

He turned, bolting for the door. His feet pounded the floor as he ran down the hallway, his legs carrying him as far as they could, faster than he thought possible. His whole body shook with fear, with the thought of what was behind him. *It's not her. It's the house. Just the house.*

But as he ran, he could still hear her voice.

"Cody... don't leave me..."

The door slammed behind him, cutting off her voice. He collapsed against the wall, his chest heaving, his whole body trembling. His mind was racing, his breath coming out in sharp, uneven gasps. The house... it was using her. Twisting her into something wrong. Something that wasn't her.

But what if... what if it was her?

His hands were still shaking, the flashlight barely flickering in his grip. He had to find the others. Had to keep moving. But Sarah's voice still echoed in his mind, lingering like a ghost, and he couldn't shake the feeling that, somehow, some part of her was still there.

Chapter 29: Helen Morrow

Sam and Alen stood frozen in the hallway. The air had gone cold, and the darkness around them felt thick, like something alive. That wet, slithering sound had stopped, replaced by an unnatural silence that wrapped around them like a noose. The woman stood at the far end of the hall, her broken body swaying slightly as she stared at them with hollow, sunken eyes.

"Who the hell is that?" Sam whispered, his voice trembling as he pointed his flashlight toward the figure. It flickered weakly in the darkness.

Alen's throat tightened, a cold sweat forming on his skin. The woman's face was bruised, her wrists raw, her neck bent at a horrific angle. She didn't move, didn't speak, just stared at them, her eyes black and empty.

Suddenly, the world around them shifted. Alen's vision blurred, his heart racing as he blinked and found himself standing in a different place, a different time.

Helen Morrow got out of bed to check on her son Thomas, as she found him sleeping peacefully in his bed, as she stepped back into the hallway, she saw her husband just standing there, "Robert, did I wake you?" Robert didn't say anything, just walked into the unused bedroom. Helen fallowed and as she stepped into the bedroom, there was Robert, but something about him was wrong. He hadn't spoken, hadn't even acknowledged her. Just led her here. Now she was in the room, and the air felt heavy, suffocating. The room smelled damp, like rotting wood, and something else, something metallic. The hairs on her arms stood up as a wave of unease washed over her.

"Robert?" she whispered, taking a step forward. He was standing with his back to her, his body stiff, unmoving. Something was off about him. She could feel it deep in her gut.

She reached out, her fingers trembling as they grazed his shoulder. "Robert, what's wrong?"

The moment her hand touched him, he turned, too fast, too violently—and what she saw wasn't her husband.

His face, twisted, grotesque, was stretched in an unnatural grin, his skin tight like it was being pulled over a skull that wasn't his own. His eyes were too dark, too deep, like black holes swallowing everything. His mouth, wide and sharp, grinned down at her, and before she could scream, his hand shot out, wrapping around her throat like a vise.

Helen gasped, her fingers clawing at his wrist as she tried to pull away, but the grip was too strong. His touch burned, ice-cold and suffocating. He lifted her off her feet effortlessly, her legs kicking as he dragged her toward the bed. The room spun around her, her vision blurring as she fought to breathe, but no air came.

She tried to scream, but it came out as a strangled choke. Her lungs felt like they were on fire, her vision darkening at the edges as the creature's hand squeezed tighter. He slammed her onto the bed, the impact knocking the breath from her chest, her body bouncing against the mattress.

For a moment, she thought it might stop, but then his hands were on her again, cold, brutal. They gripped her wrists, pulling her arms above her head, and before she could process what was happening, ropes appeared, wrapping tightly around her wrists and tying her to the bedposts. She thrashed, her body writhing, but the more she struggled, the tighter the ropes became, cutting into her skin.

"Robert!" she screamed, panic rising in her throat. "Please, stop!"

But this wasn't Robert. This was something else, something dark and monstrous wearing his face. The creature grinned wider, stepping back to admire its work, its eyes gleaming in the dim light.

Helen's arms ached, stretched painfully tight above her head. She tried to pull herself free, but the ropes only dug deeper into her wrists, the skin breaking, blood dripping down her arms. She sobbed, thrashing against the bed, her legs kicking out as she tried to free herself.

The creature watched her struggle, its head tilting, that sickening grin never leaving its face. Then it moved again—fast, too fast. It grabbed her leg, twisting it violently. The sound of her bone snapping echoed in the room, followed by a scream that tore from her throat, raw and full of agony. Her leg bent in a way it should never have bent, the bone poking through the skin, blood spilling onto the bed.

Helen's vision blurred with tears, her breath coming in short, ragged gasps as the pain seared through her. She tried to kick with her other leg, but the creature caught it easily, pulling her down until her back arched unnaturally, the ropes pulling her arms tighter until she felt her shoulders pop. The pain was unbearable, blinding. She screamed again, her voice hoarse, her throat raw.

The creature wasn't done. It leaned over her, its face inches from hers, its breath hot and sour, smelling of decay and rot. Its cold fingers wrapped around her neck again, pressing down hard, cutting off her air. Her eyes bulged, her lips turning blue as she struggled to breathe, but all she could do was gasp uselessly, her lungs screaming for air.

Her body twitched violently, her muscles spasming as the creature twisted her again, her spine bending, cracking under the force. The sound of bones snapping filled the air, sharp and sickening, and her body went limp, hanging from the bedposts like a broken doll.

Helen's vision faded, the pain slipping into numbness as her mind began to shut down. Her last thought was of Thomas—her sweet boy, sleeping just down the hall, completely unaware of what was happening to his mother. She wanted to scream his name, wanted to warn him, but her voice was gone, trapped in her throat.

And then everything went black.

Alen snapped back to the hallway, his breath coming in short, frantic gasps. His chest felt tight, his heart pounding so hard it felt like it was trying to break through his ribs. He blinked, his vision clearing, and found himself staring at the woman again—the woman who had once been Helen Morrow.

Her body was bruised and broken, her neck twisted, her wrists still raw and bloody. Her dead eyes locked onto his, and she took a slow, shuffling step forward.

Sam's voice cut through the fog in his mind. "Alen... what the fuck just happened?"

Alen couldn't answer. He couldn't speak. His throat was dry, his heart still racing. Helen took another step toward him, her hand twitching as it reached out for him.

"You'll die here," she whispered, her voice broken and raspy. "Just like me."

Sam grabbed Alen's arm, yanking him back, but Alen couldn't tear his eyes away from her. Her body jerked forward, the wet, slithering sound following her every movement.

"We gotta get out of here, man!" Sam's voice was frantic, but Alen was frozen in place, the vision of Helen's brutal death replaying over and over in his mind.

Suddenly, the floor beneath them creaked, the walls groaning as the house shifted around them. The ground cracked, splitting open, separating them from the ghost of Helen Morrow. The cold air rushed in, and the wet, slithering sound grew louder, filling the hallway.

Sam pulled Alen, dragging him toward the door at the end of the hall. "Come on! Move!"

Alen stumbled, his legs weak, his mind reeling from the vision. But he moved, his body on autopilot, following Sam as the house twisted and groaned around them.

Behind them, Helen's voice echoed through the darkness. "You'll die... just like me."

Chapter 30: A Way Out

Sarah's legs were on fire, muscles burning from the constant running. Her breath came in ragged, uneven gasps as she sprinted through the twisting hallways of the house. She couldn't get away. No matter how fast she ran, every corridor looked the same. Every wall seemed to close in, squeezing her, pulling her deeper into the maze.

The house was alive. She could feel it breathing, its pulse vibrating beneath her feet, in the floorboards, in the walls. It wanted her.

"Cody!" she screamed again, her voice raw, but the sound was swallowed by the endless dark. The hallway stretched on, too long, too narrow. No answer. Nothing but the echo of her own voice.

Her flashlight flickered, the light barely holding on. "Come on, you piece of shit," she muttered, slapping it against her hand. The beam flared for a second, then dimmed again, casting crooked shadows on the walls.

Her heart was pounding so hard she thought it might burst out of her chest. Her throat was dry, her legs shaking. She wiped her sweaty palms on her jeans, trying to steady her breath, trying to calm the rising panic that clawed at her insides.

Then, she saw him.

Cody.

He was standing at the far end of the hallway, his figure shadowed but unmistakable. He was slumped, his face hidden, but it was him. It had to be him.

"Cody!" she called out, relief flooding through her, washing over the fear that had been gripping her chest like a vise.

Cody lifted his head, his eyes wide with recognition. His mouth opened, and for a second, she thought she heard him say her name.

"Sarah!"

He started running toward her, his footsteps quick, the sound of his boots echoing in the silence. She sprinted to meet him, her legs barely holding her up. When they reached each other, he grabbed her, pulling her into his arms, squeezing her so tight she thought her ribs might crack.

"Sarah," Cody gasped, his breath hot against her hair. "fuck. I thought I lost you."

She buried her face in his chest, gripping him like a lifeline. He was here. He was safe.

"I thought I was alone," she whispered, her voice cracking. "I thought... I thought I'd never see you again."

"You're not alone," Cody said, his voice shaking but firm. "You'll never be alone again. I promise."

She pulled back a little, looking up at him. His face was pale, his eyes too wide, but she could feel his body trembling. He was scared too. "What do we do, Cody? We have to get out of here."

He nodded quickly, too quickly, his hands still gripping her arms. "I found it," he said, his voice low but urgent. "I found a way out. We can leave, Sarah. We can leave this fucking place."

Her heart skipped, a flicker of hope sparking in her chest. "You found it? You really found a way out?"

"I did." His hand tightened around hers. "Come on. We don't have much time."

Without another word, Cody started pulling her down the hallway, his pace quick, his hand gripping hers tight. Sarah followed, her legs barely keeping up with him. The hallway twisted and turned, the walls shifting, warping. She kept glancing behind her, half-expecting something to leap out of the shadows. But Cody didn't slow down. He was leading her, and she trusted him.

They stopped at a door. Just a normal, old wooden door, like all the others in this twisted place.

Cody pushed it open with a slow creak, motioning for her to go inside. "This is it."

Sarah hesitated, her hand still in his, her heart thudding in her chest. "This is the way out?"

Cody nodded, his eyes too dark, his smile too tight. "Yeah. Go on, Sarah."

Something in her gut twisted, but she stepped inside anyway. The room was small, almost claustrophobic. The walls were bare, the floor covered in dust. There was a single chair in the corner, old and broken, and a cracked mirror leaning against the far wall. No windows. No light except from her flickering flashlight.

Sarah's stomach knotted up tighter. This didn't feel right.

"This is where we leave?" she asked, her voice shaky. "I don't... I don't understand."

Cody stepped in behind her, closing the door with a soft click. The sound made her jump. "Yeah, Sarah," he said softly, too softly. "This is where we leave."

Her breath caught in her throat. Something about his voice was wrong. Off.

She turned to face him. "What do you mean? We're leaving together, right?"

Cody's smile stretched wider, too wide. The skin around his mouth cracked, dark blood trickling down his chin. His eyes—those weren't Cody's eyes anymore. They were black, empty pits of darkness.

Her blood ran cold.

"Cody?" she whispered, her voice barely audible.

His smile split open, his lips tearing, revealing sharp, jagged teeth underneath. His face twisted, the skin peeling away like old paint, revealing something monstrous underneath. Rotting flesh, the smell of decay filling the room.

"This is where you leave," the thing said, its voice no longer Cody's. It was deeper now, guttural, like rocks grinding together. "Like I said, this is where you leave."

Sarah stumbled back, her heart racing, her hands trembling. "No... no, this can't be real..."

But it was. The thing standing in front of her wasn't Cody. It was something else, something that had been pretending to be him. Its face peeled away, revealing glistening muscle, torn and bloody. Its eyes were nothing but black pits, its teeth long and jagged.

"I'm not Cody," it hissed, stepping closer. "Cody's gone. He's been gone."

Her breath came in sharp, shallow gasps. She pressed herself against the wall, her legs shaking so badly she could barely stand.

"Please... please don't..."

But the thing didn't care. It leaned in, its breath hot and foul, like rotting meat. Its tongue flicked out, long and slick, and it licked her cheek, the touch cold and slimy, leaving a trail of saliva on her skin.

"You taste good when you're scared," it whispered, its voice a low growl. "The house is so hungry, Sarah. And it's your turn."

Before she could react, the demon grabbed her by the arms, its fingers digging into her flesh, sharp claws piercing her skin. She screamed, kicking out, but it was too strong. It yanked her forward, slamming her into the wall. The impact knocked the air out of her lungs, her vision blurring as pain shot through her body.

"Please!" she screamed, her voice cracking. "Someone help me!"

But no one was coming.

The demon's grip tightened, and it leaned in close, its tongue flicking out again, tasting her fear. "You're mine now," it whispered, and then it struck.

It yanked her arm behind her back with a sickening crack. Her shoulder dislocated, the bone snapping under the pressure. She screamed, her body convulsing in pain, but the demon didn't stop. It pulled again, harder this time, and with a brutal, wet rip, her arm tore away from her body.

Blood sprayed across the room, splattering the walls, soaking the floor. Sarah collapsed to the ground, her body shaking, her breath coming in shallow, ragged bursts.

Her arm lay on the floor beside her, torn and mangled, nothing but a mess of muscle and blood.

But the demon wasn't done.

It grabbed her leg, its claws digging deep into her thigh, and with one swift motion, it yanked her leg clean off. The sound of muscle tearing and bone snapping filled the room. Blood poured from the wound, pooling beneath her, soaking into the floorboards.

Sarah's body convulsed, her vision dimming. She couldn't move. She couldn't even scream anymore.

The demon crouched over her, its claws running through the blood that soaked the floor. It licked its fingers, its eyes glowing with hunger. "The house thanks you, Sarah," it whispered, its voice low, satisfied.

With one final motion, the demon reached down, grabbing her head, its claws digging into her scalp. It twisted her neck, and with a brutal snap, everything went black.

Chapter 31: The House Closes In

Sam couldn't shake the image of Helen Morrow's body—broken, twisted like a ragdoll. Her dead eyes stared through him, still pleading, still filled with pain. He had felt it all. The crunch of her bones, the tearing of her skin. It clung to him, seeping into his mind. The house was alive, and it was playing with them.

Alen's voice snapped him back. "What the fuck did we just see, Sam?" His words were sharp, panicked, and he was pacing the room like a caged animal. "That wasn't real, right? Tell me that wasn't fucking real."

Sam swallowed hard, his throat dry, heart hammering in his chest. He didn't know how to explain what he had just seen—what he had felt. "It was her," he finally muttered. "Helen. I saw her die. It was like… I was there."

Alen ran a trembling hand through his hair, his breathing fast and uneven. "Don't say that shit, man. Don't even think about it. We need to get out of here, before—before that happens to us."

Sam nodded, but something inside him had already shifted. He couldn't unsee what the house had shown him. The memory of Helen's twisted limbs, the way her life had been snuffed out like it was nothing, clung to him. It felt like the house was already starting to close in around them, squeezing their fear tighter.

"Yeah, let's go," Sam said, trying to push the dread down. "We need to find the others."

The room felt smaller, the air thicker. The walls seemed closer, like they were bending inward, watching, listening. Sam's skin prickled as they turned toward the door, but something was wrong. There was no door. No way out. Just a solid wall where the door had been moments ago.

"Where the fuck is the door?" Alen muttered, moving toward the spot where it had been. He pressed his hands against the wall, pushing, but it didn't budge. "It was right here. Right fucking here!"

"It's the house," Sam whispered, more to himself than to Alen. "It's... changing."

"No shit, it's changing!" Alen's voice cracked as he banged his fists against the wall. "It's trying to trap us, Sam! We have to move. We have to get out of here."

They turned away from the blocked-off door and started moving again. The hallway stretched out in front of them, impossibly long and dark. The flickering beam of Sam's flashlight barely cut through the shadows. The walls groaned around them, like the house was alive, shifting and pulsing with every step they took.

Sam's legs felt heavy, his pulse pounding in his ears. Every sound—every creak of the floorboards, every distant whisper—made his heart jump. The house was toying with them. He could feel it, in his bones, in his gut. It wasn't just a haunted house. It was something more, something darker, more alive than any of them had realized.

"This is all wrong," Alen muttered, his eyes darting around. "It feels like we're being watched."

"We are," Sam said quietly. "The house is watching us."

"Yeah? Well, it can fuck right off," Alen growled, his hands clenching into fists.

They quickened their pace, the air growing colder with every step. The walls seemed to shift and warp as they moved, bending in ways that made no sense. Sam's skin prickled, every nerve in his body screaming at him to stop, to turn back. But there was nowhere to go but forward. No way out. Only deeper into the house.

Then, they heard it.

Whispers.

Soft at first, barely audible, like the wind brushing against the walls. But it grew louder, more distinct, until Sam could make out words—Helen's voice.

"Sam..." the whisper called, broken and distorted. "Help me..."

Sam stopped dead in his tracks, his heart slamming against his ribs. His breath caught in his throat. He turned to Alen, his voice barely a whisper. "Did you hear that?"

Alen nodded, his face pale. "Yeah. I heard it."

The whispers grew louder, curling around them like smoke, seeping into their ears, their skin. Helen's voice was all around them now, broken and desperate. Sam felt his stomach twist, bile rising in his throat. He wanted to scream, to run, but his feet were glued to the floor.

"Sam," the voice called again, closer now, more urgent. "Help me... please."

"We need to go," Sam muttered, his voice shaky. "We need to get the fuck out of here. Now."

Without another word, they broke into a run, sprinting down the twisting hallway. The walls groaned louder, shifting and creaking as they passed, the whispers chasing them, pushing them forward.

But no matter how fast they ran, the hallway seemed to stretch on forever. Every corner they turned, every door they tried to open, led them back to the same place. The house was playing with them, leading them in circles, trapping them.

"It's a fucking maze!" Alen gasped, his breath coming in ragged gulps. "We're going in circles. There's no way out."

Sam didn't answer. His mind was racing, trying to piece together some kind of plan, some kind of escape. But nothing made sense anymore. The house was changing faster than they could move, bending reality around them like it was nothing.

They kept running, their footsteps pounding against the wooden floor, their breath harsh and labored in the freezing air. The walls began to warp, stretching and twisting in unnatural ways, like they were alive.

Then, without warning, a wall slammed down between them.

Alen hit it first, his shoulder crashing into the solid wood with a thud. He staggered back, clutching his arm. "Sam!" he yelled, spinning around. But Sam was gone. All that was left was the cold, dark wall separating them.

"Sam!" Alen yelled again, pounding his fists against the wall, panic rising in his chest. "Sam, where the fuck are you?"

No answer.

He pressed his ear against the wall, listening, but there was nothing. Just silence. Cold, crushing silence. His breath came faster, his hands shaking. He couldn't hear Sam. He couldn't even tell if Sam was still on the other side.

"Fuck," Alen muttered, his voice trembling. "Fuck, fuck, fuck!"

He banged on the wall again, harder this time, but it didn't move. Didn't budge an inch. The house had separated them, just like it had separated Cody and Sarah.

Alen's heart raced, his thoughts spiraling. He felt trapped, suffocated. His hands were shaking as he tried to catch his breath. "Sam," he called out again, but it was quieter this time, more desperate. "Sam, where the fuck are you?"

On the other side of the wall, Sam had stopped running. He turned around, expecting to see Alen right behind him, but all he saw was the long, empty hallway stretching back into the shadows.

"Alen?" Sam called, his voice echoing down the corridor. Nothing. Just the soft creak of the floorboards and the distant hum of the house breathing.

His chest tightened, and his grip on the flashlight faltered. "Alen!" he shouted again, louder this time, but still nothing. The hallway was empty, the doorways dark and silent.

Sam's pulse quickened. He spun around, searching for any sign of Alen, but the walls had closed in, twisting the path behind him into something new, something unfamiliar. His breath came in sharp, panicked bursts. The house had taken Alen.

"Shit," Sam muttered, wiping the sweat from his forehead. His flashlight flickered, the light barely cutting through the shadows. Alen was gone, and Sam had no idea where to go. The house was shifting faster now, bending reality around him like it was playing a sick game.

He took a shaky breath, trying to steady himself. Stay calm. Think. But it was hard to think when the walls felt like they were closing in, when every step he took felt like it could be his last.

Suddenly, he heard it again. Footsteps. Slow, deliberate, echoing down the hallway behind him.

Sam's blood ran cold. He turned, shining his flashlight into the darkness, but there was nothing there. Just shadows, twisting and shifting in the flickering light.

The footsteps grew louder, closer.

Sam swallowed hard, his heart pounding in his chest. Something was coming.

Chapter 32: Unseen Shadows

Cody's breathing was uneven, his flashlight shaking in his hand as he moved through the dark, winding hallway. The air felt thick, like it was pressing in on him from all sides, and the house... the house felt wrong. Alive. His mind raced with everything he'd just read in that godforsaken diary. Robert Morrow's desperate scrawl was still fresh in his mind—how the house had changed, twisted, and taken his family one by one.

"Alen? Sarah? Sam?" Cody's voice was rough, cracking as it echoed through the empty hall. His pulse thudded in his ears as he waited, straining to hear anything—a voice, footsteps, anything.

Nothing.

He cursed under his breath, glancing down at the diary clutched tightly in his hand. The worn leather cover felt rough against his palm, the name "Robert Morrow" barely visible anymore. It detailed the Morrow family's nightmare in this house, how it had driven Helen insane before killing her in some twisted, brutal way. How Robert had fought to protect them, only to be split in two. *Goddamn place tore him apart,* Cody thought, his stomach churning. Thomas, the youngest... he might have been the only one to make it out, but even that was just a faint hope—no solid proof.

Cody swallowed hard, trying to shake the horrific images the diary had planted in his head. *We're next.*

"Sarah? Alen?" His voice cracked again as he called out, louder this time. He took a shaky step forward, his flashlight flickering. *This place is trying to fuck with us.*

Then, he saw her.

Sarah was standing at the far end of the hallway, her back to him, her silhouette barely visible in the dim light. His heart thudded in his chest, relief flooding him for a moment. But something was off. She wasn't moving.

"Sarah?" Cody called, his voice edged with tension. He moved toward her, cautiously at first, but quickening his pace when she didn't respond. "Sarah, where the hell have you been? I've been looking all over for you!"

Still, she didn't turn.

Cody slowed, his gut tightening. "Sarah?" His voice was quieter now, unsure. He stopped just a few feet behind her, close enough to feel how cold the air had gotten around her.

Slowly, Sarah turned, but her movements were stiff, almost mechanical. When she faced him, her eyes looked distant, empty, like she wasn't really there. But she smiled, a small, tight smile that didn't quite reach her eyes.

"I got lost," she said softly, her voice flat. Too flat.

Cody frowned, his stomach doing flips. "Yeah, well, I thought I lost you for good back there." He took a breath, trying to push down the unease that was creeping into his chest. "You seen Alen or Sam?"

Sarah shook her head slowly, the smile still there but frozen in place. "No. I thought they were with you."

Cody ran a hand through his hair, his nerves fraying at the edges. "Fuck. We need to find them. This place... Sarah, I found something." He hesitated, the words catching in his throat. His hand tightened around the diary. "It's bad."

Sarah's eyes flicked to the diary in his hand, her expression eerily calm. "What did you find?"

Cody swallowed hard. "It's Robert Morrow's diary. It talks about how the house started changing. How it drove Helen mad, how she was killed... in a really fucking gruesome way. And Robert, he tried to protect the family, but... he couldn't. The house tore him apart. Literally." He stopped, the images from the diary flashing in his mind. He forced himself to keep going. "Thomas, the youngest... he might've found a way out. Barely. But I'm not sure, Sarah. We need to get outta here. We're not safe."

Sarah's smile didn't falter, but something about her felt... off. "Do you think we can leave?"

The question hit Cody like a punch in the gut. He stared at her, feeling a chill crawl down his spine. "Of course we can. We just need to find Alen and Sam, and we'll figure it out, the diary said something about a door in the basement" But even as he said it, doubt gnawed at the edges of his mind. Was there really a way out? Or were they just the next victims of this place?

Sarah nodded slowly, her eyes lingering on the diary again. "Maybe." Her voice was quiet, too quiet.

Cody's pulse quickened. Something wasn't right. He started walking, gesturing for her to follow. "C'mon, we'll check downstairs. Maybe they're in the kitchen or the dining room." He tried to sound confident, but the unease was gnawing at him now, refusing to go away.

They moved together down the hall, the oppressive silence pressing down on them. Cody kept glancing at Sarah from the corner of his eye. She seemed... off. Too calm, too detached, given everything that had happened. It was like she wasn't really with him.

"You okay?" Cody asked, glancing at her again as they descended the staircase.

Sarah looked at him, her head tilting slightly. "I'm fine, Cody. I'm just fine, are you ok?"

Her voice was soft, but something about it set off alarm bells in his head. He forced a laugh, trying to shake off the creeping dread. "no im not ok, I'm fucking scared outta my head Sarah."

They reached the bottom of the stairs, and Cody swung the flashlight across the room, searching for any sign of Alen or Sam.

Nothing. The air down here felt even thicker, colder, like the house was closing in around them. His heart pounded in his chest as they stepped into the living room, the shadows seeming to stretch and shift as the light hit them.

"Where the hell are they?" Cody muttered, frustration bubbling up. "They can't just disappear."

Sarah was quiet beside him, her eyes following the beam of the flashlight as it cut through the dark. She didn't seem worried. She just stood there, too still, too calm.

"Sarah... you sure you didn't see them?" Cody asked, his stomach flipping again. Something wasn't right.

Sarah smiled that strange, empty smile again. "No. I've been with you, Cody, all along I've been with you, right by your side"

His heart stuttered. "What the hell does that mean?"

Her smile widened, her eyes darkening. "You found that bastard's diary, didn't you?"

Cody blinked, his throat tightening. "What?"

"You shouldn't have read it, it wont help you anyway" she continued, stepping closer, her voice lower now, colder. "But it's too late now."

Cody's pulse raced, his breath catching in his throat. He took a step back, gripping the diary like it was the only thing keeping him grounded. "Sarah, what the fuck is going on?"

Her face twisted, the smile stretching into something grotesque. Her eyes darkened further, turning black, hollow pits. "You're not leaving, Cody," she whispered, her voice no longer hers. "You're never leaving, none of you are, you all mine,"

Cody stumbled back, his stomach lurching with pure terror. His mind scrambled, refusing to accept what he was seeing. "You're not Sarah."

The thing wearing Sarah's face grinned wider, baring sharp, jagged teeth. "No," it purred, stepping closer, its voice dripping with malice. "But I wear her well, don't I?"

Cody's breath came in short gasps, panic surging through him like a tidal wave. He took another step back, his heart thudding painfully in his chest. "What... what are you?"

The demon's grin twisted further, its eyes gleaming with dark amusement. "This house takes what it wants. And now it wants you, Cody, it wants all of you."

Before he could react, the demon lunged at him, its cold, bony fingers wrapping around his wrist. The touch burned, searing into his skin like fire. Cody screamed, yanking his arm back, but the skin where it had touched him blistered, raw and painful.

The demon laughed, a deep, guttural sound that echoed through the room. "Run, Cody," it hissed, leaning in close. "Run while you can."

Cody didn't hesitate. He turned and bolted, the diary still clutched tightly in his hand. His feet pounded against the floor as he ran, his breath coming in ragged gasps. Behind him, the demon's laughter followed, growing louder, more twisted, as the house itself seemed to come alive, warping and twisting around him.

Chapter 33: The Changing House

Sam's footsteps echoed through the hallway, each one sounding louder than the last in the dead silence of the house. The air felt thick, heavy, like it was pressing down on him, making it harder to breathe. His flashlight flickered, casting jittery beams of light on the warped, peeling wallpaper. Every inch of this place felt wrong, like it was alive and watching him. Waiting.

The house moaned, a long, low sound that seemed to come from deep within the walls. Sam froze, his heart pounding in his chest, breath catching in his throat. He stood still, straining his ears.

Then, he heard them.

Whispers. Faint at first, like a breeze brushing past his ear, but they grew louder. More insistent. It was as if the walls themselves were whispering to him, calling him closer, begging him to listen.

"Sam..." The voices hissed, his name barely audible, but enough to send a chill racing down his spine. He swung his flashlight around, eyes darting from shadow to shadow. There was no one there. Nothing but the house. But the house is alive. The thought settled in his mind, cold and sharp.

The whispers grew louder, overlapping, a cacophony of voices—some angry, some pleading, some laughing. His hands trembled as he gripped the flashlight tighter, trying to keep his breaths steady. "Focus. It's just the house messing with you," he muttered to himself, but the words didn't offer much comfort. His skin prickled, and the hair on the back of his neck stood on end.

He kept moving, each step feeling heavier than the last. The hallway stretched out before him, longer than it should've been. It felt like he'd been walking for hours, but the end never seemed to get closer. His flashlight flickered again, plunging the hallway into near darkness for a moment before sputtering back to life.

Then, all at once, everything changed.

The walls seemed to warp, bending inward, and the air grew impossibly thick. The hallway twisted, its shape shifting right before his eyes. The house groaned, the sound rising from the floorboards like a deep, guttural growl. Sam's heart hammered in his chest as he staggered back, eyes wide, the floor tilting under his feet. The whole house was shifting—bending reality itself.

And then he saw it.

A door. It hadn't been there before, hadn't even existed a moment ago, but now it was standing at the end of the twisted hallway. Dark wood, slightly ajar, with light spilling out from the crack.

Sam's breath caught in his throat. He wasn't sure what was worse—the fact that the house was changing or the fact that he felt an overwhelming pull to go through that door. His pulse quickened, his palms slick with sweat as he moved toward it, the whispers growing louder with each step.

His fingers brushed the door, cold against his skin. It creaked open wider, revealing the faint outlines of a staircase beyond. Narrow and steep. The servant's stairs.

Sam swallowed hard, his flashlight beam cutting through the dark space ahead. The kitchen was down there. He could smell it now—faint hints of old grease and mildew. His stomach churned as he took a cautious step onto the stairs. The wood groaned beneath his weight, the sound echoing up the narrow space.

The door creaked shut behind him, trapping him in the stairwell.

His breath came quicker now, every nerve in his body screaming at him to turn back, but his feet kept moving, step by agonizing step, the air growing colder with each descent. The whispers followed him down, creeping into his mind, their voices slithering into his thoughts.

"This place will never let you go..." one voice hissed, clear as day. Sam jerked his head around, eyes wide, but the stairwell was empty. He was alone. Or at least he thought he was. The walls seemed to breathe, the narrow space closing in tighter around him.

"Come closer," another voice whispered, soft and sinister, brushing against his ear like icy breath.

Sam's heart pounded so hard it felt like it might burst from his chest. His flashlight flickered again, and this time, it didn't come back on. Darkness swallowed him whole. He froze, his mind racing. No. No, no, no, not now. His hands fumbled for the light, shaking as he tried to fix it, but the damn thing wouldn't cooperate.

The whispers closed in, growing louder, overlapping, filling the stairwell with a suffocating sound. He could barely think, barely breathe. Cold sweat dripped down his back as his fingers finally found the switch, flicking it desperately.

The flashlight sputtered back to life, weak, but it was enough.

Sam sucked in a sharp breath, his hands trembling as he held the beam steady. The door at the bottom of the stairs loomed in front of him now, so close, but somehow, it felt miles away. His heart raced, his mind screaming at him to turn back, to run, but something was pulling him forward. Something he couldn't resist.

He reached for the door, his fingers shaking as they wrapped around the cold, metal knob. He could hear the faint hum of the kitchen beyond, the distant drip of a leaky faucet, the low hum of the old fridge. Everything felt too quiet, too still, as if the house was waiting, watching.

Sam swallowed hard, steeling himself before he pushed the door open.

It swung inward with a loud creak, revealing the dark, empty kitchen beyond. The smell hit him first—the unmistakable scent of something long rotten, like food that had been left to decay for days, mixed with the sharp tang of metal. Sam's stomach churned, bile rising in his throat as he stepped inside, the floor creaking beneath his boots.

The kitchen looked wrong. Off. The appliances were covered in a thick layer of dust, the cabinets hanging off their hinges, the countertops cracked and splintered. This was not the kitchen they had when they first came to the house. His breath came in short gasps as he moved farther into the room, the weight of the house pressing down on him. The whispers were still there, lingering at the edge of his mind, taunting him, but they were quieter now. Waiting. Watching.

Sam's flashlight flickered again, casting quick, fleeting shadows across the walls, and in the brief darkness, he thought he saw something. A figure, just for a second, standing in the corner of the room, watching him. His heart stuttered, and he whipped the beam of light toward it, but there was nothing there. Just empty space.

His hands shook as he swept the light across the room again. Nothing. *I'm losing it.* The thought made his blood run cold. The house was playing tricks on him, bending reality, making him see things that weren't there. Or worse, making him miss things that were.

He swallowed hard, forcing himself to move, his feet dragging across the kitchen floor. He needed to find the others. He needed to get the hell out of here before the house swallowed him whole.

Chapter 34: The Return

Thomas stood in front of the house, his heart pounding in his chest. The old, worn facade of the house hadn't changed much in all these years. It stood just as he remembered it, casting an imposing shadow on the road that led to its entrance. He couldn't believe he was here, after all this time. At 43 years old, the memories of that night still haunted him. But now, something was pulling him back, drawing him to the place he had sworn he would never return to.

He hesitated for a moment, staring at the front door. It was unlocked. Thomas frowned, his hand hovering over the doorknob. He didn't expect that. The house had been sold a few years ago, but no one had lived in it for long. Still, an unlocked door felt like an invitation. Like it had been waiting for him.

With a deep breath, Thomas grabbed the knob and slowly pushed the door open. It creaked on its hinges, just like it had years ago, and he stepped inside. The familiar smell of old wood and dust filled his lungs, but there was something else—something new.

His eyes scanned the living room, and to his surprise, everything looked... fresh. The walls were newly painted, the floorboards polished. Renovation tools were scattered about: a bucket of paint, brushes, a tarp covering part of the floor. Someone had been fixing the place up, working to restore the home. But there was no sign of anyone now.

"Hello?" Thomas called out, his voice echoing through the empty house. He waited, but there was no answer.

He took another step inside, glancing around. The house was back to normal—or at least it looked like it. Everything was clean, neat, as if the years of abandonment had been wiped away. But Thomas knew better. The house was hiding something. He could feel it. The air was thick, heavy, and a chill ran down his spine.

"Is anyone here?" he called out again, louder this time.

Silence.

His heartbeat quickened as he walked farther into the room, his footsteps soft on the newly polished floor. The house was playing tricks on him. It didn't want him to see what was lurking beneath this shiny new surface. Not yet.

He moved cautiously through the living room, taking in every detail. New curtains hung by the windows, and the chandelier overhead gleamed in the sunlight streaming through the glass. But it felt wrong. Too normal. Too perfect.

Suddenly, a gust of cold air rushed past him, sending a shiver down his spine. Thomas stopped in his tracks, his breath catching in his throat. His pulse quickened as he looked around, but there was no one there.

And then, out of nowhere, a voice—deep and menacing—rumbled through the house, shaking the very walls. It was a voice that seemed to come from everywhere and nowhere all at once.

"Welcome back, Thomas. We've been waiting for you."

The words echoed through the room, filling every corner, creeping into his mind. His heart raced, pounding in his chest as his eyes darted around the room. The voice was thick with malice, dark and heavy with something ancient. Something far worse than he had ever imagined.

Before he could react, the front door behind him slammed shut with a deafening bang.

Thomas spun around, eyes wide, his body frozen in place. The house had him now.

And it wasn't going to let him go.

Chapter 35: Sam and Thomas

The kitchen looked exactly like it had when they first got there—too clean, too normal. Sam stood still for a second, trying to shake off the dizziness. Everything felt off. He hadn't seen anyone since he and Alen got separated. The house had swallowed his friend somewhere, twisting the halls, the rooms, until nothing made sense.

A creak came from the living room, making Sam's heart jump. He hadn't heard the door open, and the house had been messing with them the whole time. It wasn't like someone could just walk in. He moved slowly toward the sound, each step feeling heavier than the last. When he reached the doorway, his breath caught.

There was a man, standing near the front door. Sam's pulse spiked. Who the hell was this guy? He hadn't seen anyone else, and now a stranger just appeared out of nowhere?

"Who are you?" Sam's voice came out sharper than he intended, but he couldn't help it. "How the hell did you get in?"

The man's eyes flicked toward Sam, calm and steady. "The door was unlocked."

Sam's eyebrows shot up, his head spinning. "No, it wasn't," he said, shaking his head. "We tried it, and it wouldn't budge. Windows won't break either. We've been stuck here for hours."

The man seemed unfazed by this, his expression unreadable. He took a step forward, offering his hand. "I'm Thomas," he said, his voice low. "Thomas Morrow."

Sam felt the name hit him like a gut punch. *Morrow.* His blood ran cold, and a sharp, vivid image flashed through his mind—Helen

Morrow, her body twisted, torn apart right in front of him and Alen. They had tried to stop it, but there was nothing they could do. The house had ripped her apart.

"Helen Morrow?" Sam's voice wavered, his mind racing.

Thomas nodded, his face darkening. "She was my mother."

Sam stood there, stunned, his mouth dry. "We... we saw her die. The house... it took her."

Thomas's jaw clenched, and he looked down for a moment before meeting Sam's eyes again. "I know," he said, his voice tight with pain. "It took my dad too. And now it's trying to take you all."

Sam felt a sickening wave of dread wash over him. "What the hell is going on in this place?" His voice was barely above a whisper.

Thomas let out a slow breath, his gaze sweeping the room, as if the house itself could hear him. "It's not just the house. There's something worse here, something alive. It feeds on people. My family... we weren't the first. And you won't be the last."

Sam's skin prickled, a cold sweat breaking out across his forehead. "So it's not just a haunting?" he asked, trying to make sense of it all.

"No," Thomas said, shaking his head. "It's far worse than that."

The silence between them grew thick, like the air itself was suffocating. Sam's mind flashed to Cody, Sarah, and Alen. They were still out there, somewhere in this twisted nightmare, and now it wasn't just about finding them—it was about getting out alive.

"We've got to find them," Sam said, urgency creeping into his voice. "Cody, Sarah, and Alen. They're still in here."

Thomas nodded, his face grim. "If they're still alive, we don't have much time. The house won't let them go easily."

Without another word, the two of them moved deeper into the house. The hallway stretched before them, dim and cold, the walls closing in. Sam's heart raced as he kept glancing around, waiting for the house to shift again, to pull them somewhere they didn't want to go. The silence was suffocating, the air thick and heavy.

"Sarah!" Sam called out, his voice echoing down the hall. "Cody! Alen!"

Nothing. Just the oppressive quiet.

They moved from room to room, checking every corner. Everything looked normal—too normal. Like the house was trying to trick them, hiding the horror beneath a thin layer of normalcy. The kitchen, the dining room, the study—all pristine, like no one had ever set foot in them. But the air felt wrong, heavy with something they couldn't see but could definitely feel.

"This place..." Sam muttered, running a hand through his hair, his nerves on edge. "It's fucking with us."

Thomas looked back at him, his face hard. "It likes to play games before it strikes."

Sam clenched his fists, frustration boiling up inside him. The house wasn't just trapping them—it was toying with them, like a predator playing with its prey. He called out again, his voice hoarse from the tension. "Cody! Alen! Sarah!"

Still nothing.

The stairs loomed ahead of them, and Sam's stomach twisted with dread. He didn't want to go up there, but he knew they had no choice. He glanced at Thomas, who nodded, and they began to climb.

Each step felt like walking deeper into the jaws of some unseen monster. The air grew colder, and Sam's heart raced faster with every creak of the old wood beneath his feet. His mind flashed back to the last time he'd seen Alen—just a few hours ago, but it felt like a lifetime. Then Sarah had disappeared, too, her voice calling to them one minute, gone the next.

They reached the top of the stairs, where a long hallway stretched out before them, doors lining either side. Each one slightly ajar, as if daring them to look inside.

Sam hesitated, his pulse quickening. "Where do we even start?"

Thomas glanced down the hallway, his expression unreadable. "It doesn't matter," he said quietly. "The house will take us where it wants us to go."

Sam swallowed hard, dread creeping up his spine. He moved to the first door, pushing it open slowly. His heart pounded in his ears, bracing for whatever horror might be waiting inside.

But the room was empty. Just a small bedroom, untouched by whatever darkness lurked in the house.

The next room was the same. And the next.

With every empty room, Sam's frustration mounted. They were wasting time, and the house was loving every second of it. It was waiting for them to break.

They reached the final door at the end of the hall, and Sam stopped, his breath catching in his throat. He could feel it—the house was leading them here.

He pushed the door open, and the room beyond was dimly lit. But something was there. A figure, sitting in the corner.

Sam's heart raced. Was it Alen? Cody? He stepped forward, his hand shaking as he reached for the figure.

But no. The room was empty.

Just a trick of the light.

"Fuck," Sam muttered under his breath, stepping back, his hands trembling. The house was playing with them. It was getting inside his head.

Thomas stayed by the doorway, his face pale and grim. "We need to move," he said quietly. "Before it's too late."

Sam nodded, his throat tight with fear. The others were still out there, somewhere, but the house wasn't going to let them find them easily.

And deep down, Sam knew—the worst was yet to come.

Chapter 36: The Horrors Unveiled

Cody moved through the dim, suffocating hallways, his heart pounding like a drum in his chest. He had been searching for Sam, Sarah, and Alen, but the house twisted around him, the walls closing in, turning each corner into a dead end or a new nightmare. Every step he took seemed to pull him deeper into something dark, something alive.

"Sam? Sarah?" His voice cracked in the stale air, barely carrying through the oppressive silence.

Nothing.

The house groaned, creaking like it was breathing, watching him. His hand trembled as he wiped sweat from his brow, and his breath hitched. He had to keep moving, had to find the others.

Suddenly, he turned down a hallway and stopped dead. There it was, an old wooden door, worn and out of place like it had been there for centuries. Cody's stomach knotted as a sense of dread crept up his spine. The door didn't belong here, but the house wanted him to find it.

He swallowed hard, forcing his legs to move toward the door. His fingers hovered over the rusted handle for a moment, his mind screaming at him to leave, to turn back. But he had to know.

With a shaking hand, he twisted the knob and pushed it open.

The smell hit him like a fist to the gut—coppery, thick with the stench of blood and decay. His stomach twisted violently, bile rising in his throat. The dim light of his flashlight flickered across the room, and when it landed on the floor, Cody's heart stopped.

There, lying in a pool of dark, congealed blood, was Sarah.

Her body was mangled beyond recognition. Her leg had been torn away from her body, her arm ripped from its socket, both thrown across the room like discarded pieces of a broken doll. Blood stained the floorboards, seeping into the cracks, and her head... her head was twisted at an unnatural angle, neck snapped so far that her lifeless eyes stared back at him.

Cody gagged, stumbling backward. "No... oh, fuck, no!" The bile in his stomach rose higher, and he collapsed to his knees, vomiting onto the floor as the horror of what he was seeing sunk in. His body trembled, hands shaking uncontrollably as he tried to wipe his mouth. His breath came in ragged gasps, his mind spinning in a whirlwind of shock and disbelief.

He couldn't tear his eyes away from Sarah's mutilated body, the image searing itself into his brain, etched into his mind forever.

And then he heard it.

The laughter.

Low, dark, and guttural. It started as a whisper, barely audible, but it grew louder, filling the room with a mocking, malevolent sound. Cody's skin crawled as the laughter seemed to come from every corner of the room, circling him like a predator toying with its prey.

He staggered to his feet, his body trembling as he backed away from Sarah's mangled remains. His breath came in shallow bursts, and his vision blurred as panic gripped him.

"Get the fuck out..." he muttered to himself, his voice barely a whisper. But his feet wouldn't move. He was frozen, trapped by the weight of the terror that consumed him.

The laughter grew louder, crueler, as if the walls themselves were alive with it, feeding on his fear. Shadows danced along the edges of his vision, moving and twisting, mocking him with their dark shapes.

Then, the voice came. Deep, smooth, and filled with malice, it cut through the laughter like a blade.

"You can't leave, Cody. You know you want Sam, we know your desires and your thoughts, what you want to do with him, you want his love, so pathetic, but we can make that happen."

Cody's blood ran cold, and a wave of nausea hit him hard. His breath hitched, and his body locked up, but his mind screamed at him to run. He had to get out. He had to run.

The laughter stopped abruptly, the room falling into an eerie, suffocating silence.

Without thinking, Cody spun on his heels and bolted for the door. His heart hammered in his chest, his legs trembling beneath him, but he didn't stop. He slammed into the hallway, the door banging shut behind him with a deafening thud. His footsteps echoed through the narrow hall as he ran, his breath coming in panicked gasps.

The house seemed to shift around him, twisting and warping as he raced down the corridor, the shadows closing in, but Cody didn't care. He had to get away. He had to get out.

Chapter 37: False Salvation

Alen stumbled through the dimly lit hallway, his legs barely carrying him. The house had twisted around him, warping every corner into a new nightmare. He had been calling out for hours, his voice hoarse from shouting, his mind slowly unraveling. Sam, Cody, Sarah—he hadn't seen any of them in what felt like a lifetime, and the crushing weight of fear was closing in on him.

Then he saw him.

Sam.

Standing at the far end of the hallway, just standing there, like nothing had happened. Like the house wasn't alive and playing with them. Alen's heart leapt in his chest, relief hitting him so hard it almost made him dizzy.

"Sam!" Alen's voice cracked as he broke into a half-run, stumbling toward his friend. "Thank fuck, man. I thought—" His breath came out ragged, his heart racing. "I thought I lost you."

Sam stepped forward, a small smile tugging at his lips. His eyes met Alen's, calm and steady, like none of the horrors in this house had touched him. Alen felt a rush of relief wash over him. His body sagged a little, the tension draining from his muscles. He wasn't alone anymore.

"I'm here," Sam said softly, his voice as steady as his gaze. "Been lookin' for you too."

Alen reached him, barely stopping himself from falling into Sam. His breath came in uneven gasps, his hands shaking. "Shit... I thought I was losing it, man." He ran a hand through his sweat-soaked hair, trying to calm his racing heart. "This place... it's fucking with us. Doing shit. I don't even know how to explain it."

Sam nodded, his eyes still fixed on Alen, that same soft smile never leaving his face. "Yeah, I know. But we're good now. Just need to get out"

Alen blinked, the relief still pounding through his veins, but something gnawed at the back of his mind. Something about Sam's voice, about the way he was standing, felt off. No, he told himself, shaking his head. He was just freaked out. This was Sam. He was here. That's all that mattered.

He took a deep breath, his stomach still twisted in knots. "We need to find the others and get the hell out of here."

Sam's smile widened just a bit, his eyes never leaving Alen. "Don't worry about the others" he said, his voice lower now. "I'm sure there just fine"

Alen's heart skipped a beat. There was something wrong in the way Sam said it, something that sent a cold chill crawling up his spine. His stomach churned, but he ignored it, convinced that it was just the house messing with his head.

"Yeah, okay..." Alen muttered, but the doubt was creeping in now, worming its way into his mind.

Sam stepped closer, his eyes gleaming in the dim light. "The others are fine Alen," he said, his voice almost playful, but there was something darker beneath it. "I made sure of that."

Alen took a step back, his pulse racing. "What... what the fuck are you talking about?" His voice trembled.

Sam's smile twisted, stretching wider than it should have. His eyes, there was something wrong with his eyes. They were too dark, too hollow, like there was nothing behind them.

Alen's heart pounded in his chest, a surge of cold terror washing over him. "Sam?" he asked, his voice barely a whisper.

The thing that wore Sam's face stepped forward, its grin warping into something grotesque, something inhuman. "You know you want this house," it whispered, its voice no longer Sam's. "We can make that happen."

Alen stumbled backward, his breath catching in his throat. His entire body screamed at him to run, but he couldn't move. He was frozen in place, his mind spinning. This wasn't Sam. It had never been Sam.

"Stay the fuck away from me!" Alen shouted, his voice cracking as he backed away, his hands shaking.

But it was too late. The thing moved faster than he could react, its hand wrapping around his throat in a brutal grip. Alen's eyes widened in shock, his hands flying to his neck, desperately trying to pry the fingers away, but the creature's grip was like iron. He could barely breathe. His vision blurred as panic surged through him, his heart racing out of control.

"You can't leave, Alen," the demon growled, its voice now a deep, menacing rumble. It leaned in close, its breath cold against his skin, sending a shiver down his spine. "We can make all your dreams come true," it hissed, its lips brushing against his ear. "Fix up this old rotting house, and you can sell it... oh wait, you can't sell it, you'll be dead, you'll be a part of it, oh it wants you so bad Alen."

Alen's lungs burned as he struggled to draw in air, his vision going dark at the edges. He tried to scream, tried to fight back, but his strength was fading fast. The demon's laughter echoed in his ears, cold and mocking, and Alen's body shook as he realized there was no escape.

With a savage motion, the demon threw him to the floor. Alen hit the ground hard, the breath knocked out of him. His ribs screamed in pain, and he gasped, trying to suck in air. But before he could even sit up, the demon was on him again, slamming its foot down on his chest, pinning him to the floor like he was nothing.

"Please..." Alen whispered, his voice barely audible, his body trembling with pain and fear.

The demon laughed, a cruel, hollow sound that echoed through the hallway. It grabbed Alen's arm, twisting it behind his back until the bones snapped, the sickening crack echoing in the empty space. Alen screamed, his vision going white from the blinding pain. He tried to move, but the demon was too strong, and his body was betraying him, his strength sapped by the agony coursing through him.

"We can fix this house up nice," the demon cooed, its voice dripping with malice. "Make it real pretty for you, new windows fresh paint, after all you did say that it was a fixer upper."

Alen's mind spun, lost in the sea of pain. He could feel the bones in his arm grinding together, his ribs barely able to take in air. His vision blurred, and for a moment, he thought he might pass out. But the demon wasn't done. It was playing with him.

With one brutal motion, the demon grabbed Alen by the head, its fingers digging into his scalp. The pressure increased as it twisted his neck, the sound of bones snapping filling the air. Alen's world went dark as the demon tore his head clean from his body, blood spraying onto the wooden floor.

The demon held the head for a moment, staring into Alen's lifeless eyes with a satisfied grin "Well I guess you can start fixing it up now Alen" Then it tossed the head aside like garbage. Alen's body crumpled to the floor, a lifeless heap, blood pooling beneath it.

The hallway fell silent, except for the steady drip of blood from Alen's severed neck, hitting the wooden floorboards with a soft, rhythmic splatter.

The house seemed to settle, the walls closing in just a little tighter, as if satisfied with its latest offering.

Chapter 38: Unraveling Fear

Cody ran, his legs burning, his heart hammering so hard it felt like it was about to burst from his chest. His breath came in ragged gasps, and no matter how fast he ran, the air around him felt thick, like the house itself was closing in on him, squeezing him from all sides.

The hallway stretched on forever. The walls shifted, groaning like they were alive, and every shadow felt like it was reaching out for him. He could still see it—Sarah, her broken body, blood everywhere. Her limbs... they were scattered across the room, like some sick fucking joke.

His stomach churned. The bile rose up in his throat, but he swallowed it down and kept running. His mind was racing, fragmented thoughts bouncing around like pinballs. Where the fuck was everyone?

His foot slipped as he turned a corner too fast, and before he knew it, he slammed straight into someone.

"Whoa, shit!" a voice yelled.

Cody stumbled back, his vision spinning, heart still racing. His eyes focused, and there they were, Sam and a amn Cody did not know. They looked just as messed up as he felt.

"Cody!" Sam grabbed him by the shoulders. "Where the hell have you been, man? What's going on?"

Cody's chest heaved, his mouth opening, but the words got stuck in his throat. His whole body trembled as he tried to get it out, tried to say what he'd just seen.

"It's, Sarah... she's..." Cody's voice cracked, and he swallowed hard, trying to get his breath under control. "She's dead, man. She's fucking dead!"

Sam's eyes widened, and Thomas's expression darkened. For a second, no one moved. The weight of Cody's words seemed to hang in the air like a stone.

Sam shook his head, not wanting to believe it. "What the hell are you talking about? We just—what do you mean she's dead?"

"I, I found her," Cody gasped, his words tumbling out fast, jumbled. "Her body, it was... fuck, man, it was torn apart! Her arm, her leg... it's like something... something ripped her to pieces. I don't even know... I ran. I couldn't... I couldn't handle it."

He was babbling, barely making sense, but the panic had taken over. He wasn't even sure they could understand him.

Thomas stepped forward, his voice calm but firm. "Slow down, Cody. Where did you find her?"

Cody's head jerked toward the direction he'd just come from. "Back there, in one of those rooms... just down that hallway. I can take you. You have to see... fuck, man, I don't even know if I'm seeing things right anymore."

Sam looked over at Thomas, his face pale, his lips pressed into a tight line. He was trying to hold it together, but Cody could see the cracks. They were all falling apart.

"Alright," Sam said, his voice wavering. "Let's go. Show us."

Cody turned on his heel, his legs still shaking as he started walking, Sam and Thomas following close behind. The air was colder now, and with every step, Cody's chest felt tighter. The silence pressed down on them, broken only by the soft creaks and groans of the house, like it was mocking them, enjoying the chaos it had caused.

They moved down the hallway in a tense, suffocating silence. Cody kept glancing back at Sam and Thomas, his nerves shot to hell. Sam looked like he was barely holding it together, his jaw clenched, his eyes darting around like he was expecting something to jump out at them. Thomas, though... Thomas was different. He wasn't saying much, but there was a hardness in his face, like he knew something they didn't.

As they got closer to the room, Cody's breath started to hitch. His stomach churned, the memory of Sarah's lifeless body flashing through his mind again.

Sam shot him a glance. "Are you sure about this, Cody? It can't be... Sarah... dead?"

Cody nodded, swallowing hard. "You'll see, man. I'm not making this shit up. I wish I was."

They reached the door. Cody stopped, staring at it like it was about to come alive and swallow them whole. His body tensed, fear clawing at his chest. His hand hovered over the doorknob, but he couldn't make himself touch it.

Sam stepped up next to him. "Open it."

Cody's fingers curled around the knob, ice-cold against his skin. His hand shook as he turned it, pushing the door open slowly, the hinges groaning like they were screaming.

The smell hit them first.

Blood.

The thick, metallic stench filled the room, making Cody gag. Sam covered his mouth, his eyes wide with shock. "Oh, fuck..."

Thomas stepped inside, his expression grim. His eyes scanned the room, landing on Sarah's broken body. She was still there, just like Cody had left her. Her arm was twisted away from her body, her leg missing, her head at that horrible angle.

"Oh, no... Sarah," Sam whispered, his voice trembling. He backed up a step, his eyes glued to the scene. "This can't be happening. How the fuck did this happen?"

Cody shook his head, his legs giving out as he slumped against the wall. "I don't know, man. I found her like this. I just... I just ran."

Thomas crouched down next to Sarah's body, his face tight, but he didn't touch her. His eyes flicked over the scene, taking everything in, piecing it together. He was quiet, too quiet.

Sam let out a shaky breath, his hands running through his hair. "This house... it's playing with us. What the hell is happening?"

"I don't know," Cody mumbled, his voice small. "I don't fucking know."

Thomas finally spoke, his voice low. "Whatever did this... it's still here. It's in this house. It's been watching us, playing with us, and now it's starting to pick us off."

Sam's head snapped up. "What are you saying?"

"I'm saying we're not alone," Thomas replied, standing up, his gaze never leaving Sarah's body. "And whatever's here, it's not finished with us yet."

Sam cursed under his breath, pacing back and forth like a caged animal. "This can't be happening. How do we fight this? How do we get the fuck out of here?"

Thomas turned to Cody, his face hard. "You said you ran when you saw her. Did you see anything else? Hear anything?"

Cody wiped his face, his hands trembling. "I... I thought I heard laughing. But I didn't see anything. It was just... there. Like it was all around me."

Sam stopped pacing, his eyes wide. "Laughing? Are you sure?"

Cody nodded slowly, his stomach twisting in knots. "Fuck Yeah I'm sure, I thought it was my mind playing tricks, but... it was real. I swear, Sam. Something was laughing."

The room fell into a heavy silence. The weight of Cody's words hung in the air, thick and oppressive. Sam's face paled even more, and Thomas's expression darkened.

"We need to go," Thomas finally said, his voice steady but urgent. "Now."

Sam looked at him, desperation flickering in his eyes. "Go where? We don't even know where Alen is! How do we get out of here?"

Thomas's eyes hardened, his voice cold. "We find Alen, then we get out. We don't split up again. And we don't stop moving."

Cody's breath hitched, fear gnawing at the edges of his mind. He glanced back at Sarah's body, bile rising in his throat again. "We're not making it out of here, are we?"

Thomas didn't answer.

Chapter 39: Thomas Story

The three of them stumbled down the creaky stairs, the air feeling thicker, like it had claws dragging at their skin. The living room, if you could still call it that, reeked of something foul—like a mixture of rot and mold that hit them square in the gut. Everything was wrecked. Furniture sagged like it had given up a long time ago, and the wallpaper peeled off in long strips, curling like dead leaves.

Sam wrinkled his nose, eyes darting around. "Shit, it's worse now," he muttered. "It's changed again."

Cody kicked at a leg of what used to be a chair, his nerves frayed. "Yeah, no shit," he muttered, then turned his eyes on Thomas, his voice sharp. "Who the hell are you, man? How'd you even get in here? We can't get out, no matter what we do. Doors, windows—nothing opens."

Thomas sat down, his hands shaking slightly, though he tried to hide it. "I've been here before," he started, his voice low and rough. "This place... it was my home. I lived here... with my family."

Cody blinked, taken aback. "Lived here? This place? Are you serious? This shithole?"

Sam, leaning against the wall, arms crossed, stared at Thomas with disbelief. "You're sayin' you used to live here? What the hell happened?"

Thomas looked at the floor, taking a deep breath. "It wasn't always like this. The house... it changes. It wasn't like this when we first moved in."

Cody snorted. "So what the hell happened?"

Thomas let out a long breath. "This diary... the one you found. It's my dad's. Robert Morrow. He tried to make sense of everything... everything that happened in this place."

Cody pulled out the diary, flipping it open, the pages yellowed and brittle. "This belonged to your dad?" he asked, handing it over.

Thomas took it, running his fingers over the cover. "Yeah. It was his. He kept writing in it, even when everything went to shit." He paused, eyes flickering with something dark. "It all started with my mom."

Sam frowned, leaning forward. "Your mom?"

Thomas nodded, his voice strained. "She was the first to go... I mean, the house got to her. She started hearing things, seeing things that weren't there. It got bad... real bad. We didn't know what was going on. One night, my dad and I found her."

Cody's stomach dropped, the weight of what Thomas was saying hitting him like a punch. "Found her where?"

"In one of the bedrooms," Thomas whispered. "She was tied to the bedpost... bruised, beaten. We don't know how it happened. She was tortured... like something in this house was playing with her. And there was nothin' we could do to save her."

Silence hung in the room, thick as the stench of decay.

Cody swallowed hard, his voice tight. "What... what did you do?"

Thomas's hands trembled as he gripped the diary. "We... we didn't know what else to do. The house had us trapped, just like it has you now. No way out. So, we took her body down to the basement. There was nowhere else."

Sam ran a hand over his face, trying to process it all. "So you just... left her down there?"

Thomas's voice cracked. "We didn't have a choice, man. We couldn't get out. But later... later, I found something."

Cody raised an eyebrow. "What did you find?"

Thomas hesitated, his eyes darting to the floor. "A door. An old, wooden door."

Sam said as he leaned back. "In the basement? "We need to go down there but first we need to find Alen."

Thomas shook his head. "It wasn't there when we took her down... but later, after my dad... after he was gone, I found it. It wasn't there before."

Cody shot him a sharp look. "After your dad? What happened to him?"

Thomas closed his eyes, his jaw tight. "I found him in the library. His body... he was torn apart. The house... it got him too."

Cody felt a chill run down his spine. "And the door? What about the door?"

Thomas's voice was barely a whisper now. "It was in the basement. Old, wooden, covered in dirt... like it had been hidden. I knew it wasn't there before. But it was my only way out." I put it in the diary, not sure why, I just did, and now I'm glad I did"

Sam looked at him, disbelief etched in his face. "And you just... walked out?"

Thomas laughed bitterly. "Hell no. The house didn't want me to leave. The walls started closing in, the floor shifted beneath me. But I forced my way through that door. It's the only way out."

Cody paced, his mind racing. "And you think it's still down there?"

Thomas shrugged, his eyes tired. "Maybe. This place... it changes. It hides things. But if that door's still there, it's our only shot."

Sam rubbed his hands together, his nerves shot. "So what now? We just head to the basement and hope this door shows up again?"

Thomas nodded. "Yeah. That's all we can do."

Sam shook his head. " first we need to find Alen, I'm not leaving him here"

Cody's face twisted in frustration. "of course not Sam" he looked at Thomas. "And if the doors not there?"

Thomas met his eyes, his voice steady. "Then we're screwed."

Silence fell over them, the weight of their situation crushing. Sam finally broke it. "What happened after you got out?"

Thomas let out a long, shaky breath. "I tried to tell them. The cops, the doctors... they found me wandering on the road, barely able to speak. They thought I was insane. Took me back here, but the house... it was normal. It didn't look like this. They found my dad's body, but they didn't believe me. They thought I did it."

Cody grimaced. "And they didn't lock you up?"

Thomas shook his head. "No. They sent me to a psych ward. Said I was unstable. Kept me there for years. But I never stopped thinkin' about this place... about what happened here."

Sam stared at him, eyes wide. "And now you're back?"

Thomas nodded. "Yeah. I had to come back. Someone bought the place... I couldn't let it happen again."

Cody stared at him for a long moment before looking at Sam. "So... we go to the basement?"

Sam exhaled slowly, nodding. "Looks like it, but first we find Sam, then we get the hell outta here"

Chapter 40: The Wrong Hallway

Sam's breath was shallow, the flashlight shaking in his sweaty grip. The house had gone quiet, but not in a peaceful way. No, this was the kind of quiet that felt like something was about to go terribly wrong. The air was thick, pressing in on his chest. Cody's footsteps were too loud behind him, and Thomas, trailing at the rear, hadn't said a word in a while.

"Where the fuck is Alen?" Cody's voice broke the silence, the panic creeping into his words. His usual swagger was gone, replaced by raw fear. "We've been through every room on this floor. It's like he's vanished."

Sam wiped at his forehead, his skin clammy. "He's around here somewhere. We just have to keep looking."

They were running out of places to search. Every room they'd opened had been empty, nothing but dusty, forgotten spaces that felt wrong. The kind of places you wanted to leave as soon as you stepped in.

Thomas muttered something under his breath, his voice low and dark. "This place doesn't let go."

Cody shot him a glance. "What the hell's that supposed to mean?"

Thomas didn't answer right away, just kept walking, eyes fixed ahead like he was already dreading what they'd find. "It takes what it wants. Alen... we might already be too late."

"Don't say that," Sam snapped, his voice sharper than he intended. "We're not leaving without him."

But even as he said it, the knot in his stomach tightened. The house felt like it was swallowing them up, leading them deeper into its guts. Every hallway looked the same—too long, too narrow, the walls leaning in like they were trying to trap them. And the air... it was colder now, like something was pulling all the warmth out of the room.

Then, Sam saw it.

Up ahead, something small, round, lying in the middle of the floor. At first glance, it didn't make sense. It was out of place. A splash of color in the gloom. His flashlight flickered over it.

"What the hell is that?" Sam muttered, squinting as he tried to make out the shape.

Cody, who'd been trailing close behind, stepped up next to him, narrowing his eyes. "Looks like... a ball? What the fuck's a ball doing in here and who put it there?"

Sam took a cautious step forward, shining the light over it again. It did look like a ball—a kid's ball, small and round, like something that shouldn't belong in a decaying hellhole like Alastar Manor.

"Maybe it's nothing," Sam said, but his voice sounded hollow. The ball didn't look right. His gut told him to turn around, to get the hell out of there. But they were already too close.

Thomas stayed back, watching with that same dead look in his eyes. "Guy's...It's not a ball," he muttered under his breath.

Sam didn't hear him, or maybe he didn't want to. He crouched down slightly, squinting as his light passed over the object again. It was round, sure, but something about the way it lay on the floor, too still, too lifeless...

The hair on the back of his neck prickled.

"Wait," Sam whispered, his heart starting to race. His breath hitched. "That's... no, that's not a ball."

Cody took a step closer, then froze. His face went white. "Oh, fuck no. No way."

It wasn't a ball at all. It was Alen's head.

Sam's stomach dropped, and for a moment, the world tilted. He staggered back, bile rising in his throat as he forced himself not to throw up. His flashlight beam flickered across Alen's pale, bloodied face, his lifeless eyes staring up at the ceiling. His mouth hung open, frozen in a scream that never came.

Cody stumbled back, his breath coming in short, panicked bursts. "What... what the fuck, man? That's..."

"His head," Sam whispered, his voice barely audible. "It's his fucking head."

Alen's severed head lay there, like some sick joke, surrounded by a pool of blood that soaked into the floorboards. Sam's heart pounded in his chest, his skin crawling as the reality of what he was seeing sank in. This wasn't just the house messing with them. It was worse. The house had taken him.

"Oh no... oh fuck, first Sarah, now Alen?'" Cody gasped, his back hitting the wall as he slid down to the floor, hands gripping his hair like he was trying to pull himself out of a nightmare. "This ain't real. This can't be real."

But it was. Alen was dead. His head just lying there, and his body... Sam's flashlight followed the trail of blood a few feet away, where Alen's body was crumpled in a heap, limbs bent at unnatural angles. Broken. Torn apart.

"We're next," Cody whispered, his voice shaking, his breath coming in fast gasps. "This place... it's gonna kill us."

Thomas stood still, staring at the body. His face was pale, eyes fixed on Alen's body. His mouth set in a grim line. "It's already started."

Sam shook his head, unable to tear his eyes away from Alen's lifeless face. "We need to go. We have to get to the basement. Now."

But the walls around them groaned, shifting again, closing in like the house was tightening its grip. The floor beneath their feet trembled, and the air grew even colder, thick with the smell of blood and decay.

Thomas shook his head, his voice flat, resigned. "That door's got to be there. It has to be."

Cody let out a strangled laugh, his hands trembling as he pushed himself up from the floor. "We're fucking dead. We're all dead."

Sam's breath hitched, his pulse racing. His legs felt weak, but he forced himself to stand. "No, we're not. We're getting to that door. We have to."

The house groaned again, the walls creaking as they seemed to stretch and twist around them. The hallway they were in shifted, the doorways disappearing behind them, replaced with new ones. The air was heavier now, colder. The walls were pressing in, like they were closing off any chance of escape.

Sam's heart raced, his mind spinning out of control. He couldn't stop staring at Alen's dead eyes, the way they seemed to follow him, even in death.

"We need to move. Now," he repeated, his voice trembling.

Chapter 41: The Demon's Lair

They ran. Hard. Sam's legs felt like they were on fire, but he couldn't stop. The hallway stretched out in front of them, dark and twisting, like it was pulling them deeper into some kind of living nightmare. The floor groaned under their feet, each step squelching as if the house itself was soaked through with rot. Sam's breath came in ragged bursts, his chest heaving, each inhale more painful than the last.

"Fuck!" Cody's voice cracked, barely keeping pace, but Sam didn't dare slow down.

The air was suffocating, thick with the stench of shit and rot. It hit them in waves, like they were running through an open sewer. Sam gagged, the taste of decay clinging to the back of his throat, making him want to throw up. It felt like the house had been dead for years and they were the first to disturb its rotting corpse.

"What is that?" Cody choked, stumbling. "Smells like something's been dead for weeks!"

Sam wiped the sweat off his face, struggling to stay on his feet. The smell was everywhere, clinging to his skin, making every breath a fight to keep from retching. His lungs burned from it, like he was sucking in death itself.

But it wasn't just the smell.

The air was choked with smoke. Not normal smoke—this was different, thicker, heavier. It slithered along the ground in thick, dark tendrils, curling up the walls like it had a mind of its own. It wasn't the sharp sting of burning wood or plastic. No, this was darker, fouler. The smoke tasted like sulfur, like something burning deep underground, and it clung to the walls, suffocating the hallway with its weight.

It smelled like sulfur and burning flesh, mixed with something older, something that had been rotting for centuries. Every breath was like swallowing ash, burning its way down Sam's throat. The taste of it coated his mouth, thick and metallic, like blood and death.

"Where's it coming from?" Cody wheezed, pulling his shirt over his mouth as he ran, his eyes watering.

Thomas didn't answer. His face was pale, eyes locked straight ahead, but Sam could see the fear creeping into his features. "It's the house," Thomas finally muttered, barely loud enough to hear. "It's fucking with us."

The hallway twisted, stretching further than it had any right to, the walls closing in, pressing tighter with every step. Sam's vision blurred, the smoke too thick, distorting everything around them. The floor beneath his feet felt wrong, slick with some kind of filth that squelched as they ran, the wood beneath their boots soft and rotting, like it might give way at any second.

Then Sam saw it.

At the far end of the hallway, through the thick haze of smoke, something moved. His heart stuttered. For a second, he thought he was imagining it, the smoke twisting the shadows into something worse, but then it stepped forward.

The thing was huge. Wings, massive, leathery wings, unfurled, scraping the walls as they stretched out. The demon's body filled the narrow hallway, its grotesque face coming into view through the smoke. Its red fiery skin glistened as it pulled over sharp bones, and its eyes glowed like molten steel, locked on them with a hunger that made Sam's blood run cold.

"Holy fuck..." Cody stumbled back, his voice barely a whisper.

The demon took a step forward, its wings spreading wider, scraping the walls with a sound that made Sam's teeth grind. Its mouth curled into a wide, jagged grin, the rows of broken, sharp teeth glinting in the dim light. It looked hungry. It looked like it had been waiting for them.

"The house wants you," the demon growled, its voice deep and guttural, like it was dragging itself up from the bottom of a pit. "And what the house wants, it gets."

Sam felt his blood freeze. His legs reacted before his brain did, kicking into motion. "Run!" he screamed, already spinning around.

Cody and Thomas didn't need to be told twice. They took off, sprinting down the hallway, but the air was thick, choking them with each step, slowing them down. The floor shifted under their feet, groaning like the house itself was alive, stretching out, pulling them back.

The demon's footsteps thundered behind them, growing louder, closer. Its wings sliced through the air with a sickening whoosh, the sound of something enormous chasing them down. Sam's lungs burned, his vision blurring from the smoke and the fear twisting in his gut.

"Faster!" Cody yelled, but his voice was breaking, his panic spilling over.

Sam glanced over his shoulder, and his heart almost stopped. The demon was right there, grinning, its eyes glowing brighter, its massive wings beating against the air as it closed in. They weren't going to make it.

Then, the floor dropped out beneath him.

One second he was running, the next, everything shifted. The ground disappeared, and Sam was falling, crashing down into the darkness below. He hit the floor hard, the impact knocking the breath from his lungs. For a moment, the world spun around him, everything going black.

When he finally opened his eyes, the hallway was gone. The demon was gone.

Sam pushed himself up, his arms trembling. The air was still thick with the stench of rot, but the smoke was thinner here. He blinked, trying to get his bearings. The walls were crumbling, the floor beneath him soft and cracked, like it hadn't been touched in years. He was alone.

"Cody? Thomas!" Sam's voice echoed through the empty hallway, but there was no answer. Just silence. The house had separated them.

Cody stumbled to a stop, his breath coming in ragged gasps. He spun around, wide-eyed, looking for Sam. "Where the fuck is Sam?"

Thomas stared down the now empty hallway, his face pale. "The house... it split us up."

"No shit!" Cody barked, panic rising in his voice. "He was just here, right next to me!"

Thomas grabbed Cody by the arm, trying to steady him. "We'll find him," he said, but his voice was tense, like he wasn't sure he believed it himself.

Cody shook his head, his eyes wild. "The house doesn't want us to. It's screwing with us! We're next!"

Thomas didn't argue. He just clenched his jaw and started down the hallway again. "Come on. We're not leaving him behind."

Cody swallowed hard, forcing himself to follow. The hallway groaned around them, the air growing colder, heavier, like the house was closing in on them with every step.

Chapter 42: The Demon's Game

Sam's chest heaved, each breath ripping through him like sandpaper. The house was messing with him again—stretching, bending. He was pretty sure it was trying to break his brain. One second, it felt like he was in the same room over and over, and now, this hallway, too long and too crooked, didn't make sense. His legs burned, his shirt was soaked in sweat, and the air was thick with the stench of rot. He couldn't even catch his breath. It was like every inhale was clogged with the stink of the place.

"Cody! Thomas!" he yelled, his voice echoing down the hall. It just bounced back at him, like the house was laughing.

Nothing.

Fuck.

His flashlight flickered, sputtering out for a second before coming back to life, barely lighting the floor in front of him. His legs felt like lead. His feet pounded against the ground, each step feeling heavier, like the floor was swallowing him whole. Sam couldn't shake the feeling that the house was changing while he ran, the walls squeezing in just a little closer, the floor stretching just a little longer. He wasn't sure if it was real or if his mind was just spiraling out of control. Either way, it felt like he was chasing something he'd never catch.

But he had to keep going. He had to find them.

Rounding another corner, he froze. His heart leaped into his throat.

There.

Cody and Thomas, at the far end of the hallway, turning the corner, just disappearing from view. For a second, relief washed over him. He wasn't alone. He wasn't losing it. They were right there.

"Cody! Thomas!" he shouted, louder this time, his voice cracking as it echoed back at him. They didn't stop. They didn't even look back.

Why the hell weren't they stopping?

Sam took off running again, the ground squelching under his boots, the floorboards damp and soft, making every step feel wrong. The house felt more alive than ever, groaning and creaking with every move he made. It was like the whole place was watching him, waiting for him to fuck up.

He skidded around the corner, barely keeping his balance, and saw them again. Cody and Thomas, standing at the far end of the hallway, just... standing there. They weren't moving. They were just waiting.

His heart pounded harder, something uneasy crawling up his spine. They were too still. Way too still.

But there they were, his friends. Alive. He should be glad. But something about the way they stood there wasn't right.

"Hey!" Sam shouted, waving his arm. "Wait for me!"

They didn't respond. Didn't move.

His skin prickled.

He slowed his pace, something cold settling in his gut. They were facing him, standing perfectly still, almost like statues.

They were standing too still. Too quiet.

He stopped, just staring at them from a few yards away, trying to make sense of what he was seeing. Cody's arm moved then, beckoning him. "Sam! Hurry the fuck up, man!" Cody's voice carried down the hall, sharp, urgent.

Something inside Sam wanted to run. The hair on the back of his neck stood up. He didn't know why, but something wasn't right. The air felt different, thicker somehow, like it was pressing down on him. He didn't want to get any closer.

But Cody was alive. Thomas was alive.

They were okay.

Sam swallowed the lump in his throat and forced himself to keep walking. "I'm coming!" he called out, even though every instinct in his body screamed at him to turn around and get the fuck out of there. His feet felt heavy as he moved forward, his steps slower now. The hallway was too dark, too quiet, and their faces were still hidden in shadow, but that didn't make sense either. The flashlight should've lit them up more than this.

"Sam! Come on, hurry the fuck up!" Cody waved again, more frantic this time.

Sam started jogging toward them, ignoring the creeping dread in his gut. It was just the house. That was all. The house was messing with his head again. He was tired, scared out of his mind. That's all this was.

He kept telling himself that.

As he got closer, though, the air felt... off. Almost like something was pushing against him, making it harder to move, harder to breathe. His skin tingled, and sweat dripped down the side of his face, but it was more than just the physical exhaustion. It was the way the air smelled now. There was something new to it, a sharp metallic tang beneath the rot, like blood in the air.

Something was wrong.

His steps slowed again. He was maybe ten feet away now. Close enough to see them more clearly.

That's when he noticed it.

They weren't blinking. Not once. Cody's face was still locked in that same stiff smile, that same frozen expression. Thomas didn't move either. They stood there, staring at him, too still, too perfect. Too wrong.

Sam's heart pounded harder, a cold sweat breaking out over his skin. "Guys?" he said, his voice cracking with uncertainty.

That's when their bodies twitched.

One single, jerky movement. Almost like a glitch in a video. Both of them, at the same time.

Sam froze, his breath catching in his throat.

"Guys?"

Then their bodies began to move. But not the way bodies should move. Their arms and legs twisted, their spines contorting with sickening cracks. It was Cody's voice that broke the silence, but it didn't sound like Cody anymore. It was deeper, raspier, like something was grinding the words out of his throat.

"Sam..." Cody's voice called. But it wasn't Cody's voice. It wasn't even human. "You're too slow."

Sam stumbled back, eyes wide as he watched their bodies begin to meld together. Skin stretched, bones snapped and reformed, their faces merging into one grotesque, deformed thing. Sam's stomach turned. The sound of skin tearing and muscles pulling apart filled the hallway, louder than anything else.

"No... no, no, no..." Sam whispered, backing up, his whole body trembling.

It was wrong. So wrong.

Before his mind could even process what he was seeing, Cody and Thomas were gone. What stood before him now was the demon, Its massive wings unfurled with a sickening snap, scraping the walls as it spread wide, casting deep shadows over the narrow hallway.

Sam stumbled back again, his legs barely working. His heart hammered in his chest, panic twisting in his gut. The thing grinned, its eyes gleaming with a sick hunger, its deformed body towering over him.

"Got you," it hissed, its voice rattling through the air, vibrating in Sam's skull.

Before Sam could react, the demon reached out with one clawed hand and grabbed him by the throat.

Sam gasped, his hands flying to the demon's wrist, but it was like iron, cold and unmovable. He kicked, squirmed, tried to wrench free, but the thing lifted him off the ground like he weighed nothing. His feet dangled above the floor, panic surging through his body as his breath was cut off.

"Oh, you smell like fear," the demon growled, pulling Sam closer until its face was inches from his. Its breath was hot and foul, stinking of decay and sulfur. "I've waited for this, waited so very long."

Sam choked, his vision starting to blur.

Somewhere down the hallway, Cody's scream pierced the air.

Sam's eyes snapped open, heart racing. Cody was alive?

The demon chuckled, low and dark, its voice vibrating through Sam's body. "I'm going to have fun with your soul, Sam," it hissed, its grip tightening around his throat until Sam thought his neck would snap. "Cody wanted to have fun with you too. Maybe when I get him, and that little bastard that got away all those years ago, I'll let the three of you play while I watch."

Sam's chest heaved, gasping for air. "Why didn't you just... get Thomas... when he went outside?" he rasped, barely able to force the words out.

The demon's grin twisted, eyes narrowing with a flicker of frustration. "I couldn't," it spat. "I'm just as trapped here as you are. My job is to do the house's bidding. I can't leave. Nor do I want to.

The demon's voice dropped, low and sinister. "But when the four of you came... oh, it was feeding time."

Sam's vision blurred again, his body weak and limp in the demon's grip. He couldn't fight anymore. He had nothing left.

The demon lifted him higher, its grin widening. "You never broke for Cody Sam, and he wanted you badly, but you will break for me Sam," it purred, leaning in close. "And I'm going to enjoy every second of it."

Then, the demon raised him high in the air, his eyes facing the celling, and with a sickening snap, he bent Sam into. Sams head now touched his shoes. " oh you cant die just yes Sam" The demon said as he bent Sam into. " I want you to feel every minute of this, the house is Hungry Sam, it wants you, and what the house wants, the house gets"

Sam screamed as his spine snapped, the sound of his bones cracking like dry branches. The pain was instant, white-hot and unbearable. His legs went numb. He could feel everything inside him breaking—his ribs, his spine, everything. His whole body was on fire, the pain so intense he couldn't even scream anymore.

His vision blurred, blood filling his mouth, choking him.

The demon tossed him aside like a rag doll, Sam's body hitting the ground with a heavy thud. His body twisted at an unnatural angle, blood pooling beneath him. His mind was screaming, but his body couldn't move. His head lolled to the side, staring up at the demon as it towered over him, wings spread wide, casting long shadows over his broken, shattered body.

He couldn't breathe. He couldn't speak. He couldn't do anything.

The demon grinned down at him, its eyes gleaming with victory.

"Oh your such a handsome man" The demon said. "But like the old saying goes, looks don't get you everything"

And Sam's world went black.

Chapter 43: Cody and Thomas

Cody's heart pounded so hard in his chest it felt like it was about to explode. His throat burned from the scream that had just torn out of him, but he didn't even realize he was screaming until the echo faded away into the twisting halls of the house. He saw Sam, his friend, hanging in the air, limp like a rag doll in the claws of the demon.

His legs felt heavy, trembling so bad he thought they'd give out beneath him, but he couldn't move. Couldn't speak. Couldn't do anything but stare at the scene in front of him with wide, terrified eyes. The demon's wings were massive, stretching out on either side of it, casting dark shadows across the narrow hallway. Its claws were wrapped around Sam's throat, squeezing tight, lifting him higher into the air. Sam's head lolled to one side, his chest barely rising and falling with weak, shallow breaths.

Cody wanted to move, wanted to tear Sam out of the demon's grip, but his legs were frozen. His body wouldn't listen. He was stuck, locked in place by sheer terror.

Thomas was right next to him, pale as a ghost, his eyes wide, unblinking. He didn't speak either. It was like the two of them had been turned into stone, helpless to do anything but watch as the demon toyed with their friend.

"Oh, you smell like fear," the demon growled, its voice so deep and rumbling that Cody could feel it vibrating in his bones. It pulled Sam closer, until their faces were just inches apart. Cody watched in horror as the demon's hot, foul breath washed over Sam's face, thick with the stench of sulfur and decay. "I've waited for this, waited so very long."

Sam was choking. He could barely breathe, his eyes fluttering open for a second, then closing again, his head sagging in the demon's grip. Cody could feel his own heart racing, the pulse pounding in his throat. Sam was alive, barely, but alive.

Somewhere down the hallway, Cody's scream echoed again, but it didn't matter. The demon didn't care.

The demon chuckled, low and dark, the sound vibrating through the air, crawling under Cody's skin like cold fingers. "I'm going to have fun with your soul, Sam," the demon hissed, tightening its grip on Sam's throat. The sound of bones cracking made Cody's breath catch in his throat. "Cody wanted to have fun with you too. Maybe when I get him, and that little bastard that got away all those years ago, I'll let the three of you play while I watch."

Cody's heart dropped into his stomach. He could feel the bile rising in his throat. The demon was referring to Thomas.

Sam's chest heaved as he gasped for air. His voice came out weak, barely audible. "Why didn't you just... get Thomas... when he went outside?"

The demon's grin twisted, its eyes flashing with frustration for a moment before it responded. "I couldn't," it spat, the words harsh and bitter. "I'm just as trapped here as you are. My job is to do the house's bidding. I can't leave. Nor do I want to."

Cody's stomach twisted. The demon was trapped in the house? Just like them?

The demon's voice dropped lower, growing more sinister. "But when the four of you came... oh, happy day, happy day, it was feeding time."

Thomas stumbled backward, his breath coming in shallow, panicked gasps. Cody could see the fear etched on his face, the realization that the demon wasn't just playing with Sam, it was feeding on him.

The demon lifted Sam higher, its claws digging into his skin. Cody watched in horror as the demon leaned in closer, its grin widening. "You never broke for Cody, Sam, such a shame to, you would have made such a nice couple, oh wait, your straight, poor stupid Cody" it whispered, its voice soft, almost mocking. "But you will break for me. And I'm going to enjoy every second of it."

Cody's breath hitched, his legs trembling so badly that he thought he might collapse. Do something! But he couldn't. He couldn't move. Couldn't think. All he could do was stand there, frozen, as the demon toyed with Sam like it was a game.

Then, with a sudden, brutal motion, the demon snapped Sam in half.

The sound of bones cracking echoed down the hallway, louder than anything Cody had ever heard. Sam's body bent backward in a way that wasn't natural, his spine snapping clean in two, his head nearly touching his feet. Sam screamed, but the sound was cut short, choked off by the blood spilling from his mouth. His legs went limp, his arms dangling uselessly at his sides.

Cody felt like he might throw up. His stomach churned violently, his knees buckling beneath him. He stumbled back, his hand slapping against the wall to steady himself, but it didn't help. The bile rose in his throat, burning, but he swallowed it down.

Sam's body hung limp in the demon's grip, his eyes wide and glazed over, the life slowly draining from them. He was still alive, but barely. Broken, shattered, helpless.

It lifted Sam a little higher, then with a flick of its wrist, threw him aside like he was nothing. Sam's body hit the floor with a sickening thud, his limbs twisted at unnatural angles, his head lolling to the side. Blood pooled around him, thick and dark, seeping into the floorboards. His eyes, those wide, empty eyes, stared up at nothing, blank and unseeing.

Cody's breath came in ragged gasps. He couldn't look away from Sam's body. His friend, his brother, was gone. Just like that. Dead.

But the demon wasn't done.

It bent down over Sam's broken form, grinning with satisfaction. "Oh, you can't die just yet, Sam," it whispered, its voice soft and mocking. "I want you to feel every minute of this. The house is hungry, Sam. It wants you. And what the house wants, the house gets."

Sam was too weak to scream anymore. His body was limp, broken, but the pain was still there. Cody could see it in Sam's eyes. He was still alive, still suffering.

The demon straightened, wings stretching out behind it, casting long shadows over Sam's crumpled body. It paused for a moment, staring down at its handiwork, before bending down once more. Its grin twisted into something darker, crueler.

"Oh, you're such a handsome man," it said, its voice almost sweet, but filled with mockery. "But like the old saying goes, looks don't get you everything."

Chapter 44: The Curse of Alastar Manor

The air pressed on Cody's chest like a weight, thick and cold. Every breath he took felt wrong, like he couldn't fill his lungs. His skin prickled with sweat, his eyes darting to every shadow. This place—it was alive, messing with them, twisting everything, even their heads.

Thomas stood next to him, pale as a ghost, his hands trembling. He wasn't moving, just staring ahead like he couldn't process what was happening.

"We gotta go," Cody muttered, his voice rough, sounding strange in the dead silence. "Basement. We need to get to the basement."

Thomas didn't respond. He stood there, staring at the floor like he was stuck in some loop, his eyes distant and glazed over.

Cody grabbed his arm and shook him hard. "Hey! Thomas! Snap out of it, man! We gotta move!"

Thomas blinked like he was waking from a bad dream. His face was too pale, and when he finally spoke, his voice was a faint whisper. "Yeah... I'm good," he said, though his voice trembled. "Let's just go."

Cody exhaled sharply, relieved that he had snapped out of it. But something was off. The hallway seemed longer than it had a minute ago, darker, like the walls were closing in. The smell of rot and mildew was thick in the air, and Cody's stomach twisted in knots.

"Let's get the hell outta here," Cody muttered, more to himself than to Thomas.

They hadn't taken more than a couple of steps when Thomas froze again, his eyes wide.

"Wait... look," Thomas whispered, his voice shaky.

Cody's gut sank. There, where there should've been nothing but wallpaper, a door had appeared. One that definitely hadn't been there before.

"What the hell..." Cody muttered, swallowing hard. His pulse pounded in his ears. The house was messing with them again, pulling them deeper into whatever nightmare it had planned.

Thomas, without hesitation, started moving toward the door, his hand reaching for the knob.

"Dude... don't," Cody warned, stepping back. His whole body was screaming at him not to go any further. "Let's just go to the basement, forget this."

But Thomas wasn't listening. He grabbed the knob and turned it, the old hinges creaking as the door swung open.

The room inside was cold, colder than the rest of the house. The air was stale, thick with dust, and it smelled like something had died in there. The walls were bare, and the floorboards groaned under their weight. Moonlight trickled in through a small window, casting long shadows that stretched across the floor like creeping hands.

Cody stepped in, his boots scraping the warped floorboards. The room felt off, heavier, like the air itself was watching them. His eyes scanned the room and landed on something tucked in the corner, a small writing desk.

Thomas followed his gaze. There, on the desk, was a diary. It sat alone, its leather cover cracked and faded, the edges frayed like it had been handled too many times. Cody swallowed hard, the unease tightening his chest.

"What the hell is that?" Cody asked, even though he already knew the answer.

Thomas moved toward the desk, his fingers hovering over the diary. "It's old," he muttered. "Real old. Could've belonged to anyone."

Cody didn't like the way Thomas was drawn to it, like the thing had a pull on him. Like it was whispering for him to open it.

"Wait," Cody warned. "Maybe we shouldn't mess with it."

But Thomas had already opened the cover, his eyes glued to the brittle pages.

"The writing's old," Thomas murmured, his voice distant, like he wasn't fully there. "Faded, but still readable."

Cody felt a knot form in his stomach. He didn't want to know what was inside that book, but they had come too far to turn back now.

Before Thomas could read another word, the room went ice cold, the temperature plummeting so fast that Cody could see his breath in the air. The hair on his arms stood up, and every instinct screamed to get out.

The shadows on the walls began to shift, stretching unnaturally, and then, from behind them, the sound of footsteps echoed softly down the hall.

Thomas stopped, his hands frozen on the page. "Did you hear that?" he whispered, his voice shaky, like he already knew the answer.

Cody didn't respond. His body was tense, ready to run, but his feet were rooted to the floor. The footsteps grew louder, closer. And then, a whisper, faint but clear as day.

"Cody..."

His stomach twisted. That voice.

He turned slowly toward the doorway, his heart racing in his chest. Standing there, in the darkened hall, was Sam.

Cody's blood went cold. Sam stood there, his figure faint and flickering, like a bad signal on an old TV. His eyes, wide and empty, locked onto Cody's.

"Sam?" Cody's voice cracked, barely a whisper. His throat was tight, his heart thudding in his chest. Sam couldn't be here. Sam was dead.

Sam didn't answer right away. He just stood there, watching Cody with those hollow eyes. Then, he tilted his head slightly, a soft smile on his lips.

"You don't have to fight it, Cody," Sam said softly, his voice almost sweet. "You can stay here. With me."

Cody's stomach churned, his heart racing. He loved Sam. But this wasn't him. It couldn't be. The house was playing with him, screwing with his head, making him see things that weren't real.

Cody clenched his fists, his nails digging into his palms, grounding himself. "This isn't real," he muttered, his voice shaky. "You're not real."

Sam took a step forward, his form flickering. "We can be together again," he whispered, his eyes still locked on Cody. "Forever."

Cody's breath hitched, his emotions all crashing down at once, grief, anger, guilt. His chest tightened, but he couldn't let this break him. Not now.

"No," Cody said, his voice trembling. "You're not real."

Sam's smile twisted into something darker, something cruel. "You'll regret this, Cody," he hissed, his voice cold. "You'll regret leaving me."

And just like that, he was gone. The hallway was empty again, nothing but silence and shadows stretching out before them.

Thomas stood there, his hands trembling as he stared at the spot where Sam had been. "What the hell just happened?" he whispered, his voice barely above a breath.

Cody shook his head, trying to steady himself. His heart was still racing, and his skin crawled with leftover adrenaline. "That wasn't him," he muttered, more to himself than to Thomas. "It wasn't him."

Suddenly, a figure appeared near the desk, a woman, her outline barely visible in the dim light. She was faint, flickering like Sam had been, but her presence was different. She wasn't angry or twisted. She was... watching them. Her eyes moved to the diary, then slowly to Cody.

Cody froze, his breath catching in his throat. He didn't know who she was, but she had an air of authority, something that told him she'd been connected to the house for a long time.

Her gaze shifted from Cody to Thomas, then back to the diary.

"Read it," she whispered, her voice soft but commanding, like it wasn't a suggestion.

And just like that, she was gone, fading into the shadows as quickly as she had appeared.

Cody felt the tension in the room lift slightly, but the weight of what had just happened pressed down on him hard.

Thomas swallowed, his hand shaking as he looked down at the open diary. "What... what do you think she wants us to see?" he asked, his voice weak.

Cody shook his head, trying to push the fear aside. "I don't know. But whatever's in there, it's something the house doesn't want us to know."

Thomas nodded, his fingers trembling as he turned the page.

The words blurred in the dim light, but Cody could make out the date, March 17, 1885.

Chapter 45: A Silent Record

Thomas's hands shook as he turned the brittle pages of the diary, the yellowed paper crinkling under his fingertips. Cody stood beside him, staring at the faint handwriting, the words faded with time but still legible. The air in the room seemed heavier now, pressing in on them, as if the house itself was waiting for them to uncover its dark secrets. Thomas swallowed hard and began reading aloud.

March 17, 1885

"The house is finally complete. Jonas has spared no expense in making Alastar Manor the grandest estate I've ever seen. It is beautiful, truly, but something about it feels off. Since we moved in, I've had this strange sense of unease. The house... it's too quiet. At night, the air feels heavy, like something is watching us. Jonas has been spending more time in the study, pouring over those ancient books he brought back from Europe. He says it's research for his work, but I've seen the look in his eyes. There's something dark stirring in him, and I fear it's beginning to affect this place."

Thomas's voice wavered as he continued, the tension thick between them. Cody's eyes stayed glued to the page as Thomas flipped to the next entry.

April 9, 1885

"I found Jonas in the attic again last night. He was carving symbols into the floor, muttering things I couldn't understand. The air up there is suffocating. I couldn't breathe, and the walls felt like they were closing in on me. Jonas didn't seem to notice. He just kept working, obsessed with whatever ritual he's been performing. I tried to speak to him, to tell him that we should leave this place, but he brushed me off, saying the house holds 'power' that he needs. I'm afraid for him. For us. I've heard Sebastian crying in his room, but when I check on him, there's no one there."

Cody shifted uncomfortably, the room growing colder with every word. The house seemed to be listening. Watching. Thomas turned the page, his voice a little shakier now.

May 14, 1885

"Sebastian is not himself. Our sweet boy has grown pale and sickly, his once bright eyes dull with shadows. He won't leave his room, and he speaks of 'things' he's seen in the walls. Jonas refuses to listen, saying it's nothing more than childhood nightmares, but I know better. The house is doing this to him. I can feel it. I've started hearing voices myself—whispers in the dark, calling my name. I fear for what will happen to us if we stay."

Thomas paused, his voice thick with tension. Cody glanced at him, his gut twisting. "Shit's getting worse," Cody muttered under his breath. Thomas nodded, his hands trembling as he turned the next page.

May 29, 1885

"Sebastian is gone. I can barely write these words, my hand trembles even as I try to put down my thoughts. My little boy... my baby... he's dead. I found him at the foot of the attic stairs this morning, his body broken and twisted, as though he had been thrown from some height. Blood was smeared on the walls, on the floor, everywhere. But the thing that haunts me the most is his face, his eyes were wide open, full of terror, as though he had seen something unspeakable just before he died. I screamed for Jonas, and when he saw Sebastian's body... I expected him to cry, to rage, to mourn. But he did none of those things. He just stood there, looking down at our son, and then... he smiled.

A cold, twisted smile. I don't know how to describe it. It wasn't human. It was like he found joy in it. Like this had been part of his plan all along. When I demanded to know what he had done, he said, 'The house accepted Sebastian's offering.' What kind of madness is this? My son—our son—is dead, and Jonas speaks of offerings like some pagan ritual.

I cannot understand it, and I will never accept it. I slapped him, screamed at him, but he only looked at me with those dead eyes, like he was beyond feeling anything. I wanted to run. I wanted to take Sebastian's body and leave this cursed place. But the house... it wouldn't let me. Every door, every window—it was as if they had disappeared.

I couldn't get out. I tried for hours, running from room to room, clutching my son's body in my arms, but the house kept shifting, keeping me inside. It wants us here. It wants me here. Jonas said the house has plans for us all. I don't know what he meant, but I can feel the darkness closing in. It's alive, and it's feeding off us."

Cody felt bile rise in his throat. The room seemed to close in on them, the shadows stretching and shifting unnaturally. Thomas's voice shook as he continued.

April 15, 1885

"Jonas has changed. He barely resembles the man I once loved. Since Sebastian's death, he's become even more consumed by the house. He spends all of his time in the attic, carving symbols into the walls and muttering to himself. His eyes have grown hollow, and his skin has taken on a sickly, pale tone.

He looks... monstrous. Worse than that, there's a smell about him now, like sulfur and decay. The scent follows him wherever he goes, seeping into the very walls. I still don't know what he did with Sebastian's body.

I couldn't bear to ask him. I woke one morning to find it gone. Jonas was in the attic, of course, but when I demanded to know where our son was, he refused to answer. His only words were, 'The house will take care of him now.' The house... The way he speaks of it is terrifying.

As if it's a living thing, something more than wood and stone. I cannot sleep. I hear whispers in the night, voices that call my name, telling me to come upstairs, to see what Jonas has become. I fear I already know the answer."

Cody's heart pounded in his chest as he listened. "This house... it's been like this for a long time, huh?" His voice was shaky, his breath quickening. Thomas just nodded, his face pale. He flipped to the next entry, and the room seemed to grow even colder.

June 25, 1885

"Jonas is dead. At least, I think he is. But whatever he was before, whatever soul he had, is long gone. I saw him die, or what should have been his death, in the attic. He was performing one of his rituals, speaking in that foul, guttural language he learned from those accursed books. I watched from the shadows, too afraid to stop him. And then... it happened.

The walls seemed to close in, the air thickened, and a force unlike anything I've ever felt gripped the room. Jonas screamed. His body convulsed, writhing on the floor, his bones snapping like dry twigs. His skin stretched, tearing in places, and I saw his limbs begin to twist unnaturally.

I wanted to run, but I couldn't move. I was rooted to the spot, frozen by the horror unfolding in front of me. Then came the wings. Black, leathery, and twisted, they burst from his back with a sickening crack, spraying blood everywhere. His face... it was no longer his face. His eyes burned with something unholy, his mouth stretched into a grotesque grin, fangs where his teeth once were. He had become a creature from hell itself, something born from the darkest pit of the abyss. But he didn't die.

He rose from the floor, his twisted form casting a monstrous shadow on the attic walls, and looked at me with those burning eyes. 'The house has given me new life,' he said, his voice a guttural rasp, barely recognizable as his own. I ran.

I didn't look back. I don't know what he is now, but he isn't human. He isn't my husband. He's something else. And I fear the house has more in store for me."

Thomas finished reading, his voice cracking as he reached the last words.

JULY 15, 1885

"This is my final entry. I cannot fight the house any longer. It has taken everything from me—my son, my husband. I hear them now, calling for me from the attic, telling me to join them. I can't escape. The house is alive, and it wants us all. To whoever finds this... beware. The house will not let you go."

The room seemed to exhale with those last words. Thomas closed the diary, his hands trembling. The silence that followed was suffocating. Suddenly, the temperature in the room dropped. A biting cold crept in, so cold that Cody's breath fogged in front of him. The shadows around them seemed to lengthen, stretching and twisting like dark tendrils reaching for them.

Then they saw her.

A faint figure appeared near the writing desk—a woman, her form barely solid, flickering like an old photograph coming in and out of focus. Her face was gaunt, her eyes dark and hollow. Her presence was heavy with sorrow.

Eleanor Alastar.

Cody's heart pounded in his chest as he stood frozen, staring at the ghostly figure. She didn't move toward them. Instead, she simply watched. Her eyes fell on the diary in Thomas's hands, then slowly drifted toward the door, as if she could sense something beyond them, something they couldn't see.

For a moment, Cody thought she might speak, but her mouth didn't move. Her face, pale and drawn, carried only sorrow and regret.

Her hollow eyes flickered with the faintest hint of a warning, but no words escaped her lips.

Then, as suddenly as she had appeared, Eleanor vanished, dissolving into the shadows, leaving the room colder and heavier than before.

Cody blinked, his breath coming out in ragged gasps. "What the hell was that?"

"Why didn't she say anything?" Cody muttered, rubbing his arms, trying to get rid of the freezing chill that had settled into his bones.

"I don't think she needed to," Thomas whispered, his eyes still wide as he glanced down at the closed diary in his hands. "She already said everything in the diary. Now... now it's our turn."

The weight of those words hung in the air. The house wasn't just revealing its secrets to them, it had chosen them. Just like it had chosen Eleanor, Jonas, and Sebastian. The realization hit Cody hard. They weren't here by accident. They weren't just passing through. The house had plans for them, just as it had for the Alastars.

Cody's heart thudded against his chest, the cold feeling creeping deeper. "We have to get out of here, man. We have to go now."

Thomas nodded slowly, still pale, but a strange determination flickered in his eyes. "Yeah... we're getting out. But this place... it's not going to let us go easy."

Cody turned toward the door, half-expecting it to disappear, or worse, to shift like it had before, leading them into even darker corridors. His skin prickled as the weight of the house seemed to press down harder, like it was alive, watching their every move.

The air felt thick, the shadows seemed to stretch, and the walls creaked as if something within them was shifting—stirring, ready to move.

Cody clenched his fists, his voice barely a whisper. "Let's go."

Chapter 46: The Attic

The air in the hallway felt suffocating, like the house itself was alive. Cold and thick, clinging to their skin like damp fog. Cody's heart raced as his breath came in shallow bursts, every muscle tense, his nerves on fire. He felt like the house was squeezing him, pressing down on his chest with each step, making it harder to breathe. He glanced at Thomas, whose face was ghost-white, his hands shaking so badly it looked like he could barely hold it together.

The silence between them was thick, heavy with dread. The kind of silence that came right before something terrible.

"We gotta get out," Cody muttered, barely recognizing his own voice, low and hoarse. He swiped at the sweat running down his face, even though the air was freezing. None of it made sense—he was soaked in cold sweat while the attic felt like a freezer. It made him feel like he was already too deep in something he couldn't claw his way out of.

Thomas didn't answer. His eyes were locked on something further down the hall, wide and terrified, as if his whole body had seized up. Cody followed his gaze, squinting through the dim light.

A figure.

At first, it looked like just a shadow, barely there, flickering like a dying flame. But as the shape grew clearer, Cody's stomach twisted. The figure stood still, almost ghostlike, its body flickering in and out of view, hollow and lifeless. The form of a woman. She looked gaunt, drained, like all the life had been sucked out of her.

Cody's heart slammed against his ribs as the figure solidified. Eleanor Alastar.

"Shit... it's her," Cody whispered, his mouth dry.

Eleanor wasn't trying to scare them, not like some cheap ghost in a horror story. The weight of her sorrow hung in the air around her, heavy and suffocating. Her hollow eyes locked onto them, filled with a grief that made Cody's gut churn. She wasn't just haunting them—she was warning them.

"She... she wants us to go through there," Thomas croaked, his voice barely audible.

Cody's throat tightened. "You sure about that?"

Thomas nodded slowly, his eyes darting between Eleanor and the door she was pointing at. "That door... it wasn't there before."

He was right. The walls around them seemed to shift, pushing them toward the door like the house was guiding them, forcing them. The hallway felt tighter, the space warping, closing in on them.

Without another word, they stepped forward. Eleanor's figure began to flicker again as they approached, slowly dissolving into the shadows until she was gone. Cody's stomach knotted with dread. There was no turning back now. He swallowed hard, grabbed the door handle, and pushed it open.

The stench hit them immediately, like a fist to the gut. Thick, wet rot, sulfur, and something worse—something that smelled like death, like something rotten had crawled out of the earth and had been left to fester for years.

"Shit!" Cody gagged, pulling his sleeve over his nose. "What the fuck died in here?"

The room was darker than the hallway, the air heavier. But as their eyes adjusted, the scene in front of them became painfully clear, and Cody wished it hadn't. The floor was carved—deep, jagged lines cut into the wood in the shape of a large pentagram. Symbols surrounded it, etched with force, with anger. Dusty, ancient books were scattered everywhere, their pages covered in strange, unreadable writing.

"Jonas' work," Thomas muttered, stepping inside like he was being pulled by some invisible force. His hand hovered over one of the books before he picked it up, the leather cover cracking under his fingers, almost crumbling.

Cody didn't speak. He couldn't shake the feeling that the room was alive. The air pressed down on him, making it harder to breathe, each breath feeling like he was inhaling the weight of death itself. He reached out, running his fingers along the walls—they felt wet, damp with something he didn't want to name. His hand came away slick.

"There's something else here," Cody whispered, his voice trembling.

Thomas didn't reply. His gaze was fixed on something else now, something on the far side of the room. A dark stain smeared across the floor, trailing up the wall. Cody's stomach turned as he followed Thomas's gaze.

And then they saw it.

A vision. More vivid than anything they'd seen before, like a twisted, flickering memory playing out in real time. Eleanor was there, crumpled on the floor, her body twisted and broken. Her face was contorted in fear, her eyes wide with terror as she tried to claw her way across the floor, dragging her battered body. She was desperately trying to pull herself away from something, someone.

Jonas.

But it wasn't the man from the diary. This wasn't Jonas the man anymore. His eyes glowed red, unnatural, sick. His face had twisted into something monstrous, something inhuman, his grin stretching across his face like a grotesque mask. His black, leathery wings were spread wide behind him, shadowing the room in darkness.

"No, no, no!" Eleanor mouthed, her lips trembling as she tried to crawl away.

Jonas, or whatever he had become, stepped toward her, his clawed hands stretching out, reaching for her. His voice was dark, cruel, dripping with malice.

"Where do you think you're going, my love?" he sneered, his voice a sick mockery of affection. "You never did understand, did you? This is what we were meant to be. This is our destiny."

Eleanor's mouth opened in a silent scream, her body convulsing with terror. "Jonas... please," she mouthed, tears streaming down her face. "Stop... this isn't you."

Jonas crouched beside her, his claws gently stroking her cheek, leaving thin trails of blood where his nails dug into her skin. "Oh, Eleanor... you're wrong. This is exactly who I am. The house showed me. It showed me what I could become, what I was always meant to be."

Her hands trembled as she weakly pushed at him, her eyes pleading. "You... loved me..."

Jonas grinned wider, his eyes glowing brighter. "Loved you?" He let out a low, dark laugh. "I thought I did. But love doesn't mean anything now. Power does. The house has given me everything. And you..." He gripped her throat, tightening his claws around her neck. "You're just a small piece of it."

Eleanor's eyes widened, panic setting in as his grip tightened. She gasped, her feet kicking as she tried to pull free, her fingers scratching at his arm in a futile attempt to stop him.

"Don't fight it, Eleanor," Jonas whispered, his voice soft and menacing. "Just let it happen. Let me watch you die."

Her body convulsed, her face going pale as the life drained out of her, inch by agonizing inch. Blood trickled from her mouth, her limbs twitching as she tried to breathe.

Jonas leaned in closer, his lips brushing her ear. "You were always so weak. You never could see the bigger picture. Now you'll die knowing you were nothing."

With a final, sickening snap, her neck broke beneath his hand. Eleanor's body went limp, her head lolling to the side. Her eyes, wide with terror, stared blankly into the darkness.

Jonas stood over her, his grin fading into something darker, more satisfied. He wiped the blood from his claws, flicking it aside like it was nothing. "Weak, Eleanor. You were always weak."

The vision faded, the room falling silent. Cody felt like he couldn't breathe, his heart hammering in his chest. The weight of what they had just seen pressed down on him, suffocating.

"Holy shit..." Cody whispered, his voice shaking.

Thomas was backed up against the wall, his face pale, his eyes wide with shock. "That's... that's what happened to her," he muttered, his voice barely there.

The air was thick with the smell of death, the room darker and heavier than before. The shadows seemed to pulse, waiting for something more.

Cody's eyes fell on a stack of books, there, among them, was Jonas's diary. Cody's hands trembled as he picked it up, flipping through the brittle, yellowed pages, his breath coming in shallow gasps.

March 1, 1885

"We've finally moved in. The house is everything I dreamed of—grand, perfect. Eleanor is thrilled, and Sebastian... he's happy here. I've never seen a place so full of potential, so alive. There's something about this house. The way it feels, the way it breathes. I've never felt more alive. Eleanor's already talking about decorating, but all I can think about is the attic. I know there's something up there. I can feel it calling me. I think this house has secrets, and I intend to find them."

Cody's stomach churned as he read the words, the early optimism in Jonas's writing already tainted by something darker, something twisted. He flipped the pages quickly, each entry growing more erratic, more desperate.

April 20, 1885

"I found the books in the attic. They were buried beneath the floorboards, hidden for who knows how long. They're old, older than anything I've ever seen, older than the ones I have anyway. The moment I touched them, I felt something. It was like the house was speaking to me. There's power in these books, in these symbols. They're showing me things I can barely comprehend, but I know I must study them. The house wants something, and I'm the one to give it what it needs."

The writing became jagged now, the words slashed across the page. Cody could feel the descent, like the house was swallowing Jonas whole.

May 14, 1885

"Sebastian is dead, my poor boy is dead, I think I killed him, no, it was the house, it needed him." Jonus walked around his study sometimes laughing sometimes crying, "Eleanor is beside herself; she thinks I'm a mad man, she thinks I don't care" and she is right, the house needs him, it needs all of us." He suddenly stops. "No, No I have to help her get out." Then he suddenly becomes calm letting the house talk to him in a gentle loving way. "Jonus, its ok, we have Sebastian and he's ok, we need Eleanor, we need you, don't you want power?" Jonus looks up. "I do, and that bitch will not stop me, but what about the door in the basement?" He asks in a childlike voice. "What if she finds it, what if she escapes?" The house trembles as if angry. "She will never find the door."

Cody turned the page carefully, his hands trembling. The next entry was barely legible, the writing scrawled across the page in frantic loops.

June 3, 1885

"She hasn't found the door. It's Hidden in the basement; the house showed me. It only appears when the house sleeps, when it's fed enough. I've seen it, but it's not just an escape. It's something more, a key. Eleanor is terrified of what I've become, but I can't stop now. The house is inside me, changing me. I don't need her anymore."

The final entry sent chills down Cody's spine.

July 15, 1885

"I am no longer who I was, I'm better, more powerful. The house has consumed me, twisted me into something more. The house is in control. It's always been in control. The ritual is complete. And Eleanor is dead."

The room was silent as Cody closed the diary, his hands shaking. The weight of Jonas's madness hung heavy in the air. The house had twisted him, corrupted him, turned him into the monster they had just seen.

"We need to go," Cody whispered, his voice barely audible.

Thomas nodded, wiping the sweat from his brow with trembling hands. "The basement... we need to get to the basement."

Cody's heart raced as they turned to leave, the walls seeming to breathe around them, pulsing with the hunger of the house. They didn't have much time.

Chapter 47: Descent

The stairs creaked louder than hell under their feet, every step groaning like the house was angry. Cody's lungs burned, and it felt like something was squeezing his chest, making it harder to breathe. Cold sweat ran down his neck, even though the air felt like ice. Thomas looked worse—pale as death, shaking so bad Cody thought he might collapse any second.

"We gotta move, man," Cody muttered, his voice rough, almost like it wasn't his. He swiped at his face, trying to stop the sweat. "The basement's ahead, right?"

Thomas didn't say shit. His eyes were fixed on something down the hall. Cody followed his gaze, squinting into the dim light.

There was a figure.

At first, Cody thought it was a shadow, just flickering in the bad lighting. But then it stepped forward, becoming solid. Cody's stomach dropped. Sam.

"Fuck... no." Cody's voice cracked. His heart slammed in his chest, knowing exactly what this meant.

Sam stood there, pale as a ghost, but still so familiar, so handsome and tall. His face... Cody knew every line of it, knew the way Sam's smile would pull at his lips just before a joke. But this wasn't the Sam he loved. His eyes were empty, dead, and his skin looked waxy, like something already halfway to the grave.

"Cody," Sam said, his voice soft but somehow wrong. It echoed in the hallway, carrying with it something twisted, hungry. "You don't have to leave."

Cody swallowed hard. His pulse raced in his throat. "This... this isn't real, your not the Sam I knew, your part of this fucking house." His voice shook. But his body was fighting him. He wanted to reach for Sam.

"It's me Cody, you don't have to run," Sam whispered, taking a step closer. His eyes, those empty eyes, never left Cody. "I can make you happy, I know what you want. You've always wanted me, haven't you?"

Cody's mouth went dry. His whole body tensed. He had tried so hard to bury those feelings. But now, Sam was offering himself, and it wasn't real. It couldn't be real.

"No," Cody whispered, backing up a step. "This is the house. You don't mean that."

Sam's smile was soft, almost comforting. But it was twisted, the same deadness lingering in his face. "I can make you feel good, Cody. You've been in love with me for so long... just stay. We can be together. I want you. I need you." Sam's voice dropped lower, almost seductive. "I can give you what you've always wanted."

Cody's heart twisted. His hands were trembling, his mind racing, but somewhere deep inside, the truth broke through. This wasn't Sam. The house had warped him, twisted him into something horrible.

"Hell no, Sam!" Cody's voice came out stronger than he expected. He swallowed hard, shaking his head, trying to fight off the way his heart ached. "I'm leaving. I'm not staying here with you."

The warmth in Sam's eyes dropped, replaced by something cold and vicious. His smile turned dark, his mouth curling into something cruel.

"Oh, Cody," Sam said, stepping even closer now, his voice a twisted mockery of the tenderness it had once held. "When you're dead, I'm gonna fuck your brains out."

Cody's stomach turned. A chill shot through his spine, his muscles tensing as bile rose in his throat. "Well mother fucker, you should have done that when you were alive."

"Fuck you, Sam. I'm done!" Cody snarled, the fear morphing into something hard and angry. His legs kicked into motion, and he ran toward the basement door. But Sam wasn't alone anymore. More figures were stepping out of the shadows.

Sarah was next, her face pale, her eyes wide with pain and betrayal. Her mouth opened like she was screaming, but no sound came out. Cody's chest tightened seeing her like that, her skin torn and raw, her body crumpled. They had been through everything together, and now here she was, a fucking ghost.

"Cody," she whispered, her voice breaking. "You should've saved me. Why didn't you save me?"

Cody's breath hitched. "Sarah, no. It wasn't like that." His voice cracked, guilt punching him in the gut.

"You left me," she hissed, her eyes filling with tears that streaked down her bloodied cheeks. "We were friends… you let me die."

Behind Sarah, Alan appeared, his head tilted at a sick angle, his neck a jagged mess where it had been torn off. His body was mangled, his face pale and swollen. His eyes, dark and vacant, locked onto Cody.

"You did this to me," Alan rasped, his voice gurgling as blood oozed from his neck. "You fucking left us. We're all dead because of you."

"Shit," Cody whispered, backing away from the ghosts. His head was spinning. He couldn't do this.

But then the walls started moving. The hallway groaned like the house was waking up, and the voice of the demon, rattled through the air, booming and deafening.

"You think you can leave?" Jonas's voice was dark, rumbling through the walls, the floors. "I own you. This house owns you."

The walls bent, the wood twisting like the whole damn place was coming alive. The air grew thick, so thick Cody could barely breathe, like he was being suffocated.

"Come on!" Thomas yelled, grabbing Cody by the arm. "We gotta get the fuck out of here, now!"

But Cody couldn't stop looking at Sam's dead eyes. He had loved Sam for years, and now... this.

"You won't make it," Sam's ghost whispered, taking a step closer. "You're mine, Cody. You can't escape. I'll make you feel things you've never felt before."

"Fuck that!" Cody snapped, shaking his head violently. He yanked his arm free from Sam's reach, his pulse pounding in his ears. "You're not Sam. You're nothing."

He turned, running toward the basement door, and Thomas was right there with him, stumbling, gasping, as the house seemed to close in on them. The hallway twisted, bending like it was alive, the floor shaking under their feet.

Ghostly hands burst from the walls, grabbing at their clothes, their skin, pulling them back. Cody and Thomas kicked and shoved, there mind racing. They weren't going to die here.

They slammed into the basement door, forcing it open with a loud, splintering crack. The moment they were inside, Cody slammed the door shut behind them. His chest heaved, his heart hammering against his ribs like it wanted out.

But the air in the basement was worse, thick with rot, the smell of death burning in his throat. Cody gagged, coughing against the stench.

"Fuck, man," he whispered. "We don't have much time."

Thomas nodded, his breath coming in fast, uneven gasps. "We have to find the door.

Cody fumbled for his flashlight, his fingers slick with sweat, his mind racing. The beam flickered to life, but it barely cut through the thick, living darkness that swallowed the basement. They couldn't see shit.

The house wasn't done with them. They weren't alone down here. Something moved in the shadows.

And the voice of the demon rumbled through the walls again, low and cruel. "I'm going to rip both of you apart. You'll both die here... and

I will take my sweet time killing you. Oh, the things I will do to you, Thomas I promise I will let your mother watch, as I disembowel you and make you eat your own shit." It laughed loudly. "And Cody, I will let Sam have his way with you, he will do things to you that, well... let's just say are very painful, Then I will rip your arms off, then your legs and then you head."

Then all fell silent.

Chapter 48: The Final Hour

The basement had fallen into a thick, suffocating silence. Cody's ears rang from the absence of sound, as if even the air had stopped moving. His heartbeat pounded in his chest, louder than ever in the stillness. He and Thomas stood frozen in place, surrounded by the blackness that swallowed everything around them.

For a moment, it was like the house itself had stopped breathing.

"Thomas..." Cody whispered, but his voice sounded too loud, almost foreign in the eerie quiet.

Thomas didn't answer. His eyes were wide, his chest heaving with shallow breaths, the panic still there. But everything had stopped—no footsteps, no laughter, no twisted faces emerging from the shadows. It was as if the house was waiting.

Then, without warning, the silence shattered. The walls groaned, and the air grew heavy again, thick with the weight of something dark, powerful, and furious.

The Demon appeared from the shadows, his massive black wings stretching out behind him, his eyes glowing red in the dim light. His face twisted into a grotesque grin, his voice like gravel as he spoke. "You think you can escape me? You're both mine, time to die"

Cody's pulse quickened, "What's wrong with it, it seems a bit sluggish" Cody said. "It seems weaker". He and Thomas exchanged a glance.

"You don't own us!" Cody snarled, stepping forward. "You're just a pathetic fucking man who thinks he has power, if it weren't for the house you'd be a cockroach."

The demons grin faded, replaced by a sneer of pure rage. "You'll regret those words." He lunged at them, faster than Cody expected, his clawed hand swiping at Cody's chest.

Cody barely had time to throw himself to the side, but Jonas's claws caught his arm, burning through his skin like hot iron. Cody screamed, his breath catching in his throat as the searing pain spread down his arm.

Thomas came at the demon from the side, swinging an iron pipe he had grabbed from the floor. It connected with a crack against the creatures wing, but the it barely flinched. Instead, It turned on Thomas with a snarl, backhanding him across the room with a brutal swipe.

"Thomas!" Cody yelled, his chest tightening as Thomas hit the wall with a sickening thud, crumpling to the ground. His heart hammered in his chest, and before he could move, Jonas turned back to him, his red eyes burning.

"You think you can fight me?" It growled, its voice dripping with malice. "You're nothing!"

Cody gritted his teeth, fury bubbling up inside him. He lunged at Jonas, grabbing onto one of the demon's massive black wings from behind. With a shout of pure rage, Cody pulled with all his strength, the wing tearing under his grip, black blood spurting from the tear.

The demon became weaker, it became part Jonus, part demon.

Jonas screamed in pain, thrashing as Cody ripped through the wing. "You're fucking dead, I'm going to eat you and spit your soul out!" Jonas roared, and with a savage jerk, he flung Cody to the ground.

Cody hit the floor hard, his breath knocked from his lungs. His head spun, but he could hear the demon's heavy footsteps closing in, his heart racing in his chest.

Jonas loomed over him, his hand raised, ready to strike. Cody scrambled backward, his body screaming in pain, but before Jonas could bring his clawed hand down, Thomas was back on his feet. He grabbed the pipe and swung it with all his might, hitting Jonas in the back with a loud crack.

Jonas staggered, snarling, but it didn't stop him. He turned on Thomas, his red eyes blazing. With a powerful swing of his arm, he hurled Thomas across the room, his body slamming into the wall like a ragdoll. Thomas groaned, sliding to the floor in a heap.

Cody's chest heaved as he struggled to his feet. His whole body ached, his skin burning where Jonas had touched him. But he couldn't stop. They couldn't stop.

Jonas turned his eyes back on Cody, his face twisted with rage. "You're going to die in this house," Jonas growled, his voice low and venomous. "And when you're do, your soul will be mine."

Cody's heart raced, but before Jonas could strike again, the basement shifted.

A cold gust of air swept through the room, and suddenly, figures appeared. Cody blinked, barely believing what he was seeing. It was Sam, Sarah, Alan, Eleanor, and Robert Morrow, standing tall and strong, their eyes filled with determination.

"Cody" Sam sad softly, he had a glow to him, his voice clear, steady. "We're here to help."

The demon faltered, his face twisting into confusion and rage. "No... you can't stop me!" Jonas roared, lunging at Sam. But before he could reach him, Eleanor and Robert surged forward, their ghostly forms shimmering with cold light. The spirits collided with Jonas, pushing him back.

Jonas screamed, his skin hissing and steaming wherever the ghosts touched him. His form flickered, weakened, but still powerful.

"Thomas!" Robert shouted, his voice filled with urgency. "Help Cody, get to the attic. Destroy the pentagram! That's how you stop him!"

Cody's eyes widened. "The pentagram..."

Eleanor's voice was calm but firm. "It's what binds the house to Jonas. Destroy it, and the house falls apart. The house is already weak from the spent energy it used trying to stop you, that's how we are free to fight, it has no hold on us now, Jonas is also weak."

"Go!" Sam shouted, stepping in front of Cody. "We'll hold him off!"

Jonas screamed in fury, his claws slashing through the air, trying to reach them. But the ghosts stood strong, their forms glowing with an eerie light as they pushed him back.

"Cody, come on!" Thomas yelled, grabbing Cody by the arm and pulling him toward the stairs.

Cody's legs burned as he ran, his heart pounding in his chest. The house groaned and creaked around them, the air growing thicker, darker. But he couldn't stop. They had to destroy the pentagram.

As they ran through the halls, they saw spirits from all that had died in the home, they just watched them, not interfearing.

The attic was colder than before, the air suffocating. Cody's flashlight flickered as he stumbled into the room, his eyes locking on the pentagram carved deep into the floor. The lines pulsed with a faint, red glow, casting the room in an eerie light.

Without thinking, Cody grabbed the nearest piece of shattered wood from the ground and swung it down with all his might. The wood cracked against the floor, but the pentagram didn't break.

"Come on!" Cody shouted, his voice shaking with desperation. He swung again, harder this time. The wood splintered in his hands, but the pentagram cracked, the red light flickering.

The house screamed.

The walls trembled, the floor buckling beneath his feet, but Cody didn't stop. He swung again, and this time, the pentagram shattered, the lines breaking apart into jagged cracks.

The house roared in pain, the walls groaning as if the entire structure was being torn apart. Cody could hear Jonas's screams echoing from below, the demon's voice full of rage and agony.

Without hesitation, Cody grabbed the books, the books that had started all of this, and threw them into the center of the room. He grabbed a lantern, spilling the oil over the pages, then lit a match and tossed it onto the pile.

Flames erupted, the books catching fire in an instant. The smoke rose thick and fast, the heat searing his skin. Cody stumbled back, watching as the books blackened and curled in the flames.

The house shuddered, the walls groaning louder than ever, they turned and ran back down the stairs.

When they burst back into the basement, they skidded to a stop. The spirits were still locked in battle with Jonas, but the demon was weakening. His form flickered, his wings tattered, his face contorted in pain.

"You bastards!" Jonas howled, swinging wildly at the ghosts, but his strikes were slower now, weaker.

"You're finished, Jonas," Eleanor said, her voice cold. "It's over."

Suddenly, Jonas faltered. His body flickered, and then—he changed. His wings crumbled away, the red glow in his eyes faded. And in their place, Jonas Alastar, the man he had once been, knelt there, his body broken, his face streaked with tears.

"No!" Jonas screamed, collapsing to his knees. "No, why did you do this? I had power! I was a god!"

"Not anymore, motherfucker," Thomas growled, stepping forward. He picked up the iron pipe and slammed it into the floor beside Jonas, sending a shockwave through the room.

Jonas let out one last scream as the house groaned and shook violently. And then, with one final tremor, everything went still. And Jonus was gone.

Cody stood frozen, his chest heaving, his mind reeling from everything that had just happened. But it was over. The house was dead, the demon was dead.

Sam was the first to step forward, his form shimmering softly. He gave Cody a bittersweet smile, his eyes warm but filled with a quiet sadness.

"I always knew, Cody," Sam said, his voice soft but clear. "I knew how you felt about me."

Cody's throat tightened, tears welling up in his eyes. "Sam... I'm so sorry."

Sam shook his head, stepping closer. "You don't have to be sorry. Maybe, in another time, another place, it could've been something. But..." He paused, his hand almost reaching out, though Cody could feel no warmth from it. "I love you, Cody. Not the way you wanted, but I do love you."

Tears streamed down Cody's face as his heart twisted in his chest. Sam's smile faltered for a moment, and then he said, "Thank you... for setting me free." He stepped back, his form flickering slightly, fading. "Goodbye, Cody."

Cody could barely find his voice. "Goodbye, Sam."

Sam's image shimmered, then slowly vanished into the air, leaving Cody standing there, his heart heavy and aching.

Before he could fully catch his breath, Sarah and Alan approached him. Sarah's eyes sparkled with a mix of sadness and relief as she came closer. "Cody, you were always my best friend," she said, her voice trembling. "I love you Cody."

Cody wiped at his face, his tears unstoppable now. "I... I should've been there for you."

"You were, in every way that mattered," Sarah whispered, stepping closer, her hand hovering over his cheek, though he could feel only a faint chill. "Thank you for everything. You gave me peace."

Alan gave a crooked grin, the mischievous, carefree spark he always had showing through. "Cody, man, you really did it. You saved us all."

Cody's chest heaved with emotion, his voice thick as he choked out, "I'm sorry, Alan. For everything."

Alan shook his head, waving him off. "Hey, we've all got our regrets. But you came through when it mattered." He grinned wider. "You'll always be a brother to me. See you... in a long time, hopefully."

Sarah and Alan's forms flickered, shimmering as they both began to fade into the shadows. Cody watched them go, his heart breaking and healing all at once.

As they vanished, Eleanor Alastar stepped forward. Her face, once twisted with sorrow, now held a quiet peace. "Thank you, both of you. You saved more than just my soul," she said softly. "You gave us all a chance to be free. And you stopped him."

Cody met her eyes, his throat tight. "I'm sorry for what happened to you... for what Jonas became."

Eleanor shook her head gently. "You have nothing to apologize for. You brought us peace." With a soft, grateful smile, Eleanor's form flickered and disappeared into the darkness, her long nightmare finally over.

The last to step forward was Robert Morrow. He stood tall, his stern expression softened with pride as he looked at his son. "Thomas," he said, his voice rich with emotion. "I never got to tell you how proud I am of you."

Thomas swallowed hard, his own eyes wet with tears. "Dad..."

Robert shook his head, stepping closer. "You've become everything I could have hoped for in a son. You're strong. Stronger than I ever was." He rested his hand on Thomas's shoulder, the faintest hint of warmth passing through. "You saved me. You saved all of us."

Thomas's voice cracked as he spoke. "I... I didn't know if I'd ever hear you say that."

And then from the corner of the room, a said, "Hello son, I have so missed you." Thomas looked up and there standing next to his father was his mother. She came up to Thomas and gently stroked his check. "My boy, I love you so much, Take care of yourself, never forget that we have always loved you"

"You've made us proud, son. More than you'll ever know," Robert said, his voice thick with emotion. "Take care of yourself... and take care of Cody." With a final nod, Robert and Helen Morrow stepped back, There form flickering before fading into the dim light, leaving Thomas standing there, his head bowed, tears slipping down his face.

The basement was quiet again, but this time the silence wasn't suffocating. It was peaceful.

Cody and Thomas stood there for a moment, letting the weight of everything that had happened settle over them. The house was no longer alive. No longer filled with dark, oppressive energy. It was dead, just like Jonas.

Thomas wiped his face with the back of his hand, his voice hoarse. "It's over... it's really over."

Cody nodded, taking a deep breath as he felt the tension finally release from his body. "Yeah. It's over."

Together, they made their way up the stairs, each step feeling heavier, but lighter at the same time. The walls of the house didn't creak or groan anymore, no shadows darted in the corners of their eyes. The house was just... a house now.

When they reached the ground floor, the once twisted and decayed halls were now just old and abandoned, no longer menacing. The air was fresh, no longer heavy with the weight of death and fear.

They walked to the front door, and Thomas pushed it open. Fresh air rushed in, cool and cleansing, like a breath of life after drowning in darkness for so long. They stepped out into the morning light, the sky just beginning to brighten with the first hints of dawn.

They stood on the porch for a long moment, not saying a word, just taking it all in—the stillness, the freedom. The nightmare was finally behind them.

Thomas glanced at Cody, his voice quiet. "We did it."

Cody nodded, his face streaked with tears, but there was a hint of a smile on his lips. "Yeah. We did."

There was nothing left to say. They had survived. They were free.

As they stood there, the first rays of the sun began to break over the horizon, bathing the house and the surrounding woods in a soft, golden light. It was over. Finally, after everything they had been through, it was over.

And for the first time in what felt like forever, Cody and Thomas were free.

Chapter 49: Epilogue: A New Beginning

Two years had passed since the fire that consumed Alastar Manor. The house, the demon, the horrors, it was all gone. At least, that's what Cody and Thomas believed. Life had moved on, and they had too.

The evening air was warm, and the last light of day filtered through the trees as Cody sat on the porch, watching the sun sink below the horizon. He was calm in a way he hadn't been in a long time. Beside him, Thomas stretched out in his chair, his feet propped up on the railing, a beer in his hand. They'd gotten into the habit of these porch talks—just sitting, not saying much, enjoying the quiet after everything that had happened.

Inside, Mark and Emily were cooking dinner, their soft laughter floating through the open window. It was a normal evening, something Cody hadn't known he needed until he had it again.

"You still have those nightmares?" Thomas asked suddenly, his voice low, like he didn't really want to break the peace.

Cody glanced at him, then shrugged, taking a swig from his beer. "Sometimes. Not as bad as before."

"Same," Thomas muttered, scratching the back of his neck. "But I think… I think we did it, man. We're out."

Cody nodded, feeling the truth of that settle in his chest. They had made it out alive. They had burned the house, destroyed the pentagram, set the spirits free. Sam, Sarah, and Alan, they were gone now, finally at peace. And after everything, Cody and Thomas had rebuilt their lives, piecing together something new from the ashes of that nightmare.

Cody had found stability with Mark, someone who grounded him when the memories got too heavy. Mark never pushed for answers, just offered quiet understanding, and that was enough. Thomas had married Emily, a woman with a strong, steady presence who'd helped him heal. They were thinking of starting a family soon.

"I think we're good," Cody said quietly, more to himself than to Thomas. "It's over."

Thomas smiled, tipping his beer toward Cody. "Here's to that."

The clinking of their bottles broke the silence, and for a moment, everything felt right. Normal. The way life was supposed to feel. Cody took a deep breath, savoring the calm, the soft laughter of Mark and Emily inside. The quiet between him and Thomas was comfortable, the kind that didn't need to be filled with words.

"You hear about the land?" Thomas asked after a long pause.

"Yeah," Cody replied, setting his bottle down on the porch. "Developers are moving in soon, right?"

"Next week, I think," Thomas said, nodding. "Subdivision, parks, playgrounds. Gonna be a whole new neighborhood."

Cody ran a hand through his hair, shaking his head. "Kinda weird, isn't it? All that... stuff that happened, and now they're just building houses like none of it mattered."

Thomas shrugged, taking another swig from his beer. "Nobody knows. To them, it's just land. Clean slate."

Cody thought about it for a second, but the uneasy feeling he used to have wasn't there anymore. "I guess that's for the best."

"Yeah," Thomas agreed, tipping his bottle again. "No reason for anyone to know what really happened. It's over, man. We're done with it."

They didn't talk much after that, just sat in the fading light, enjoying the simple peace of the moment. Cody glanced at Thomas, noting how much more relaxed he looked now, how much lighter. He felt it too. Maybe this was what moving on really felt like. Maybe they could finally close that chapter for good.

Inside, Mark poked his head out of the door, a grin on his face. "Dinner's ready, you two coming in or what?"

Cody smiled, pushing himself up from the chair. "Yeah, we're coming."

Thomas chuckled, standing up and stretching. "Yeah, yeah, don't eat it all."

They both followed Mark inside, the warm, inviting smells of home-cooked food wrapping around them. The door closed behind them, the porch now empty, the sky turning dark as the stars began to flicker overhead.

Meanwhile, at the construction site, the crew was working late, trying to get ahead of schedule. The sound of machinery rumbled through the air as bulldozers tore through the earth where Alastar Manor had once stood. The land had been cleared, the debris of the fire long gone, replaced with plans for a shiny new neighborhood.

Rick, one of the workers, was shoveling through the dirt near what used to be the basement. The machines groaned in the distance, but for a moment, everything felt oddly still.

As he dug, Rick thought he heard something, a faint whisper. He stopped, wiping the sweat from his brow, and turned his head slightly. It was quiet again, the low hum of the machines filling the air. But then he heard it again, just on the edge of the wind.

"Rick..."

His name. Soft, barely there. He spun around, looking over his shoulder, but the site was empty. Just the usual sounds of the crew finishing up for the day. He was about to go back to work when the whisper came again, closer this time.

"Rick..."

A chill ran up his spine, the hair on the back of his neck standing on end. He could feel the sweat drip down his temple, but he shook it off, scowling at himself. Just the wind, he told himself. He'd been working too long, that's all. The site was creepy enough without his mind playing tricks on him.

"Hey, Rick!" a voice shouted from across the site. "You gonna keep standing there, or you gonna help us finish up?"

Rick forced a laugh, his heart still racing. "Yeah, yeah, I'm coming."

He buried the unease, tossing his shovel down and heading toward the machines, but the weird feeling wouldn't leave him. The night air cooled as the crew packed up their gear for the day, and the sounds of machinery slowly died down.

The site was quiet now, nothing but darkened earth where a cursed house had once stood.

Acknowledgement

To the brave souls who dared to step into the shadowy halls of *Alastar Manor*, thank you. This tale wouldn't have existed without your willingness to face the unknown and tread where others might have hesitated. You've made these haunted walls whisper, the ghosts stir, and the darkness linger a little longer.

To each of you who turned these pages, thank you from the bottom of my heart. Your support and curiosity mean more than words can say. I appreciate every moment you've spent with this story, and I hope it's been a journey worth taking.

—Ron Trentham

Other Books by Ron Trentham

- *Crestwood High* – Romance and ghostly encounters
- *Shadows of the Reaper* – Chilling stories of mortality
- *Realities Edge* – A journey into parallel worlds
- *The Long Way Home* series – Warm adventures inspired by his beagle, Izzy
- *The Cost of Silence* – The story of James, torn between past loves and new desires

About the Author

Ron Trentham crafts his stories with a unique voice, often pulling from life's mysteries. His novels, known for their emotional depth and spine-chilling scenes, are as haunting as they are heartfelt. Whether he's wandering through wooded trails, watching a storm roll over the lake, or simply enjoying a quiet evening under the Tennessee stars, Ron finds endless inspiration in the world around him. His writing reflects his love for exploration, both of the world and the human soul, bringing readers along for a journey through both the supernatural and the deeply personal.

Milton Keynes UK
Ingram Content Group UK Ltd.
UKHW010235111224
452348UK00011B/791